The Mothman Files

To Samuel Maynard –

Edited by Michael Knost

Foreword by Jeff Wamsley

Woodland Press, LLC

PUBLISHED BY
Woodland Press, LLC
Chapmanville, West Virginia
Printed In The United States of America

© Copyright 2011, Woodland Press, LLC

ISBN 978-0-9829937-5-0

Foreword

By Jeff Wamsley

The Mothman has arguably captured the interest and curiosity of more people than any other legend. From the earliest sightings in the 1960s to present-day encounters, it's easy to understand why this creature, or being, remains one of the most fascinating subjects in paranormal history.

Speculation grows with each sighting.

Michael Knost has assembled thirteen stories on the Mothman in this book, each of which looks at this phenomenon from a different viewpoint. Although the stories are of a fictional nature, it's easy to see that the writers have studied the events and derived fantastic and sometimes terrifying ideas and conclusions from their works.

Was Mothman just a large bird, or was it something more terrifying and sinister to those caught in its path? The questions remain unanswered to this day ... *or do they?*

Jeff Wamsley
Author, *Mothman: Behind the Red Eyes*
Point Pleasant, WV

Introduction

Reports of strange occurrences and sightings in Point Pleasant, West Virginia—including the appearance of a bizarre winged apparition that became known as the Mothman—troubled this ordinarily quiet community from November 1966 to December 1967, and made headlines around the world. Mysterious lights were seen moving across the sky. Domestic animals were found slaughtered and mutilated. And John Keel—arriving to investigate the freakish events—soon found himself an integral part of the mystery.

Already an established writer, Keel began contributing articles to the *Flying Saucer Review* earlier that year and took up investigating UFOs and Fortean phenomena as a full-time pursuit. His investigations led him to Point Pleasant, where he became as much a part of the story as the Mothman itself.

Keel assembled the findings from his research into a book he titled, *The Mothman Prophecies*, in 1975. The accounts documented—including the strange phone calls he received and reports of mutilated pets—were taken from his investigations in the vicinity and climaxes with the collapse of the Silver Bridge on December 15, 1967, where 46 people sadly lost their lives.

This same book was the basis for a 2002 film adaptation staring Richard Gere. If you've only watched the movie, I encourage you to read the book. I was not impressed with the movie, but loved reading Keel's narrative. This is the first place to go if you're seeking information on Mothman. It is the origin of the Mothman.

Next, you should read the works of Jeff Wamsley, who graciously wrote the foreword for the book you are now holding, and is also the owner and curator of the Mothman Museum in Point Pleasant. His books are *Mothman: Behind the Red Eyes* (2005) and *Mothman: The Facts Behind the Legend* (2001), co-written by Donnie

Sergent, Jr.

Mothman has taken on legendary status here in the Mountain State. It seems as though everyone knows someone who claims to have seen the winged creature at some time or another. This phenomenon attracts all generations, from the youngest to the oldest, and is a subject that has produced a myriad of explanations, conspiracies, and questions.

Perhaps most alarming, many claim the Mothman visitations never stopped in the 1960s. The legend was birthed in the mountains, but now visitations have been documented around the globe. Credible eyewitnesses abound—from every region of America and South America, from Europe to Asia—of a winged beast of mammoth proportions.

I've always found the subject of Mothman to be interesting and thought it would be fun to put together a book of fictional tales surrounding the monster/being. I was curious to know what great writers could conjur up about the creature; and as I suspected, they had much to say.

I hope you'll enjoy reading these stories as much as I did. I trust the nightmares they bring will be carried to your slumber on enormous beating wings. My wish is also that the red eyes you begin to notice everywhere do not freak you out too terribly. I hope the peculiar noises you hear are not too much for you to handle. I say this because he knows you're reading about him. He knows you're thinking about him. And he knows you're afraid of him. He also knows that, like a moth to the flame, you can't resist him.

Michael Knost
Chapmanville, WV

Table of Contents

Other Great Book Titles From Woodland Press, LLC

Full Bone Moon
G. Cameron Fuller

Stories from the Hearth
Edited by Brian J. Hatcher

Specters in Coal Dust
Edited by Michael Knost

Mountain Magic
Spellbinding Tales of Appalachia
Edited by Brian J. Hatcher

Legends of the Mountain State
Ghostly Tales from the State of West Virginia
Edited by Michael Knost

Legends of the Mountain State 2
More Ghostly Tales from the State of West Virginia
Edited by Michael Knost

Legends of the Mountain State 3
More Ghostly Tales from the State of West Virginia
Edited by Michael Knost

Legends of the Mountain State 4
More Ghostly Tales from the State of West Virginia
Edited by Michael Knost

Writers Workshop of Horror
Edited by Michael Knost

The Secret Life and Brutal Death of Mamie Thurman
F. Keith Davis

West Virginia Tough Boys
F. Keith Davis

The Tale of the Devil
Dr. Coleman C. Hatfield and Robert Spence

The Feuding Hatfields & McCoys
Dr. Coleman C. Hatfield and F. Keith Davis

www.woodlandpress.com

Benefaction at 41.46 N, 50.14 W

By Chandler Kaiden

It was the timbre of the screech that brought seven-year-old Zachary Harvey to a skidding stop. Like a razor carving slate, it curled your earwax.

Zachary turned around, stuffing the rest of his biscuit into his blazer pocket. The sound had come from behind him and high up. The night, though clear and starlit, was moonless. Aft of the boat deck, the rear mast of the great ship jutted into the black sky, punctuated only by a lantern winking feebly.

Somebody's up there, Zachary thought. Though it was too dark to see it now, he knew there was a ladder that ran halfway up the mast.

He searched for a moment longer. Then, seeing nothing, he turned around again.

The boat deck looked deserted. The temperature, which had been dropping all evening, now hovered just above freezing. Dinner had been rich, as usual, and the grown-ups were all down below, in the smoking room or the library or their cabins, glutted and sluggish.

From another pocket, Zachary took a handful of almonds he'd filched from the dining room and popped them into his mouth. He started forward, munching as he walked. Pale lifeboats between their curved davits lined the edge of the deck; between them, beyond them, stretched the void that was the ocean.

The electric lights flickered.

The hissing, wriggling creature seemed to tumble out of the night itself. From the shadows ahead, near the railing, it rolled directly across Zachary's path, moving so fast it crashed headlong into the wall on his left.

Zachary cried out, spraying chewed almonds.

The creature was about the size of a puppy, only it looked more like a sinewy featherless owl than anything Zachary recognized. Its enormous eyes flashed red. It was snarled in a length of rope. Its tiny arms, like the forelimbs of a tyrannosaur, grappled with its bindings.

It's trapped, Zachary realized. *It needs—*

A second figure leapt from the darkness. Zachary took a step back, alarmed, but the newcomer didn't seem aware of him. Instead, it fell upon the creature, savagely swinging some blunt weapon.

Then Zachary recognized the long ratty hair, the tattered jacket—

Gad Husseil.

Gad was ten, traveling with his father and four brothers in steerage—though that hadn't prevented him from going wherever he pleased on the ship. Zachary had met him four days earlier, just after he and his mother had boarded, and right from the start Gad had seemed like trouble.

Now, Zachary watched as Gad beat the ugly creature with a heavy glass jug. The creature warbled and thrashed.

From somewhere behind him, Zachary heard another screech.

Then, instinct kicked in, and Zachary ran toward them.

"Gad! Stop it! Stop hitting it! You're going to kill it!"

Zachary dug his fingers into the older boy's shoulders and wrenched him backward. The creature lay trembling, mumbling strangely, watching them with enormous eyes like red half dollars.

Gad seemed to notice Zachary for the first time. He was breathless, grinning, still wielding the jug by its neck.

"Did you *see* this freaky thing?" he said, brushing a hand through his hair, sweaty even in the bitter cold. "Did you *see* it?" He laughed. "It's like a Siamese owl-bat." He laughed again and offered the bottle

2

to Zachary. "Here, have a go."

Zachary took a step to the side, so he stood between Gad and the creature, and shook his head.

"Come on," Gad said, shoving the bottle toward Zachary so its heavy bottom touched his chest. "Give the ugly freak a good crack."

"No," Zachary said. His voice sounded tiny, and though the night was windless, he heard a gentle roaring in his ears.

It struck him how much taller Gad was—a head, at least, maybe more. Zachary was runty and round. He still had a lot of baby fat on him. But Gad was fit and hard, if thin, and there on the boat deck, the two of them alone, he suddenly seemed almost a man next to Zachary.

The good-natured grin dropped from Gad's face, and a vacant, thin-lipped stare replaced it.

"I said, give it a crack."

"And I said *no*."

Zachary's heart thundered. The ocean was dead calm but the boat deck seemed to tilt. Everything looked too sharp to Zachary, too clear— as though he were seeing the world through a magnifying lens. He wished his mother were there; he wished *anyone* were.

The smirk returned to Gad's face. He thwacked his palm lightly with the glass bottle.

"Leave it alone now," Zachary said. "It's hurt. You're gonna kill it."

"So?"

"So why would you do that? Leave it alone."

"*No*," Gad said, mimicking Zachary's voice.

Zachary had a vision of the glass bottle, which was empty but very thick, shattering as Gad brought it down on top of his head.

Could he kill me with it? Zachary wondered.

"You don't even belong up here," Zachary said. "Why don't you just go away?" He tried to sound intimidating, but he felt small and scared.

"Because I don't want to," Gad said, taking a step toward him. "Now, get out of my way."

"I'm not going to let you hurt it."

Gad took another step.

"I said I'm *not!*" Zachary said.

Before he even knew he was moving, he stepped forward and shoved Gad hard in the chest, thrusting with the weight of his whole body.

It caught Gad off guard. He stumbled backwards. His arms did two pinwheels at his sides then he fell flat on his butt like a toddler learning to walk.

Zachary was so floored he couldn't move. He wanted to press his advantage—to get his hands on the bottle or, better yet, grab the creature and head down the stairs to C Deck to find his mother.

But Gad was back on his feet faster than he'd fallen, scowling so deeply the cords in his neck stood out.

"You're going to be so sorry."

He rushed at Zachary, the glass bottle held high. Zachary looked frantically for a way to dodge the blow. But there was nowhere he could go without exposing the creature.

So instead of getting clear, he covered his head with both arms and crouched.

Gad swung where Zachary's head had been earlier and struck empty air. The force of the swing cost him his grip on the bottle. It slipped from his fingers and smashed on the deck at Zachary's feet.

Zachary saw his chance. He snatched up a curved, jagged fragment. Blindly, he thrust it forward. It sliced through the air, stopping just before it pierced Gad's throat.

Both boys froze.

"Back off," Zachary said.

"Or what?"

Zachary's fist trembled. Gad looked down his nose at the glass shard. His gaze met Zachary's again.

"You don't have the—"

Zachary pushed the glass forward another inch. The tip of it touched Gad's skin, and Gad yelped and leapt backward.

He swallowed and rubbed his throat. He was breathing hard again, but this time, it wasn't from excitement.

"You listen to me, kid," he said, pointing a finger at Zachary. "I'm going to find that freak thing, wherever you take it. And when I do, I'm going to pluck its ugly eyes out with my fingers. And then I'm coming for *you*."

Zachary's pulse thumped so loudly in his ears he could barely hear the other boy's words.

"You can't hide from me," Gad said, retreating slowly. "Not even on this ship. Not even on the *Titanic*. No, I'm going to find you."

He passed beneath the farthest aft of the steamer's four towering funnels and disappeared behind the wall.

Zachary exhaled in a rush, his breath a white plume in the frigid air. He turned and knelt beside the creature. Though its body was mostly bare, patchy brown fur around its shoulders and the sides of its head formed a kind of facial ruff. It watched him intelligently; its forward-facing eyes were ruddy and deep-set.

It seemed to understand that Zachary was trying to help. It did not struggle as he used the broken glass to cut away the rope. Then he dropped the glass and, cradling the creature in the crook of his elbow, took off his thin gray blazer one arm at a time and swaddled the trembling thing.

As the coat closed around it, it began to thrash. Zachary held it close to his chest to calm it.

"Shush," Zachary whispered. "Shhh. Shush now."

What am I going to do?

Zachary knew his mother would let him bring the creature into their cabin. She wasn't like most ladies; she loved animals, and he knew she'd be proud of him when he told her how he had saved this one.

Just *how* he would get it there without a steward spotting him—and probably throwing the creature overboard—Zachary didn't know.

"But we'll figure it out," he whispered.

Though the creature's trembling was beginning to subside, Zachary was shivering now. The cold, bad enough when his blazer was on, cut right through his shirt.

He rose to go below.

And heard a soft *thump* behind him.

Gad, he thought. But he knew immediately it wasn't.

A thick, noxious smell suffused the clean sea air, and Zachary felt the fine hairs all over his body prickling.

He turned around, the sight of the monster hulking on the deck nearly brought him to his knees.

It stood twice as tall as Zachary himself. Starlight shone through membranous, veined wings stretching out from its broad back. Its blood-colored eyes flashed like signal lamps in the moonless Atlantic night. Its forelimbs were thickly muscled and each terminated in three long talons.

Zachary felt like he'd turned to stone. He would have screamed, if he could.

The monster raised its right wing; the horrendous stench intensified until it was nearly unbearable. The movement and smell attracted the attention of the smaller creature. As soon as it spotted the large one, it began to squirm.

Its baby, Zachary realized. *I've got its baby.*

He thrust the fidgeting bundle forward. The massive, silent thing extended its forelimbs to receive the baby, still wrapped in Zachary's blazer.

As soon as they touched—parent and offspring—the monster snatched it from Zachary and rocketed into the sky.

Raising one hand against the deck lights, Zachary craned his neck, turning in circles, searching for it. He spotted a flash of red—*red eyes*—near the rear mast, three-quarters of the way up, high, high above. He could almost make out the shape of its body against the stars—like a stain on the night, looking down.

Though the creature had not acted menacing, the thought of it clinging to that mast, presiding like some black angel, gave Zachary an ugly feeling.

He lowered his eyes, shivered hard, and made his way toward the second-class entrance.

The great ship was gone, its lights extinguished just moments before it vanished beneath the surface, returning the ocean to the starlit night. Floating ice—mostly growlers and a few large 'bergs—haunted the still water like craggy ghosts, tingeing the air with their mineral smell.

All around, people were screaming. They wept raggedly, crying out to the lifeboats to *come back, come back, help, save a life.*

The pain of the cold water had given way to complete numbness. Zachary wanted to hurt—hurting would have meant his body was fighting to live—but instead he felt himself slipping away.

Already his grip on the bobbing deck chair had grown limp. A strap on his lifejacket had come undone, and he floated with it up around his neck.

Got to swim, he told himself. His brain had difficulty finding the words. *Got. . . to swim. . . to the boats. . . .*

The lifeboats were out there somewhere—they *had* to be.

But Zachary knew he wasn't going to reach them. He could hardly think, let alone swim.

I'm going to die here.

He wanted to scare himself, to stoke his will. Instead, he just felt exhausted.

Where's the chair?

He hadn't been aware of letting go of it. But now it was gone. The water was littered with other floating debris. But in the dark, in his sluggish confusion, it all looked alien.

His head slipped through the neck hole of the life belt, and he got a mouthful of seawater. It was colder than freezing. It felt like a knife driven into his skull.

He kicked his legs. His head bounced back up through the neck hole, and he curled his arms over the front flap of the jacket.

His resolve didn't last long. The icy water sapped his strength, and again, he felt himself slipping.

He knew he wouldn't kick his legs anymore. It was at once a decision and a realization of an unalterable fact.

His eyelids closed.

Water lapped his chin. Then his cheeks. Then his nose. He heard gurgling as his ears slid beneath.

Then a wild shriek.

And suddenly—

He was airborne, coughing and sputtering.

His eyelids snapped open. The black Atlantic dropped away beneath him as he rushed upward, upward. Strange, green firelight glittered upon the water below like the sunrise sparkling off the ocean, only much too early and on the wrong horizon.

He saw but was too numb to feel the powerful arms that encircled his body. The bitter wind screamed and howled, beating his soaked clothes like sails, freezing them stiff. Despite the wind, he smelled the rotten odor of the thing that clutched him close.

He tried to look up and could not raise his head against the airstream.

Then they were plummeting—down, down, down, shooting toward the water.

Zachary glanced up.

Two ruddy eyes met his.

And he crashed into the middle of the lifeboat.

The violence of his landing rocked the boat. Around him, people shouted and swore. Seawater washed over the floor.

"Esther, dear, give me that bathrobe. Just for a minute. We'll get it right back to you, dear," an old woman said, and then Zachary felt thick cloth around his shoulders.

"Boat ahoy!" A man's voice, distant, echoed over the water.

Someone pinched Zachary's chin and pried open his mouth, feeding him biscuit crumbs.

"Are you all right? Look at me, son."

He opened his eyes and saw a dark shape among dark shapes in the wavering lantern light. He let his eyelids slide shut again.

He felt the warmth of human hands on his frozen back.

"*How?*" Another man's voice, close beside him. "He didn't come over the side, did he?"

"He *fell* in. From the sky."

"He can't have done. You must have—"

"I seen it, too!"

"It's a miracle."

For Zachary, the biscuit crumbs were the miracle. The human hands, the miracle.

Hours later, aboard the rescue ship—the sight of his mother, the miracle.

Blue Flame

By Bev Vincent

"What does that one say?" Vicky asks.

Her older brother, Burt, holds the cardboard packet at an angle to try to catch some light. A layer of greasy dirt coats the living room windows after years of exposure to noxious fumes from the nearby coal-powered electric-generating station, blocking out most of the afternoon sun's rays. The boxes stacked around the room like pillars, disrupting the dim glow of the pole lamp in the corner. After Grandpa died, Nana Wilkerson turned into a hoarder, buying things from late-night infomercials, much of it still in its original shipping packages.

"Silver Bridge, I think," Burt says. "There's a date, but I can't make it out."

"Sounds boring," Vicky says. They're taking a break from sorting through Nana's belongings. A few mementos they want to keep, but anything else they can't unload in a yard sale on the weekend will be donated to Good Will. What's left of the house after the scavengers strip it will be mowed down by men with bulldozers like it's made of paper and matchsticks, and dragged off to a landfill. Soon, nothing will remain but a patch of neatly mown grass, like the rest of Cheshire.

"Ready to get back to work then?" Burt asks.

Vicky looks around the room. They've been at it for three days, and there's still so much to do that she feels overwhelmed. The job fell to them because their mother was gone, again. Off with another man or in jail somewhere. Shoplifting, vagrancy, public intoxication, solicitation—she's done it all. They have no way to let her know that *her* mother died, as if she cares about any part of her family. Their father washed his hands of her after the last time she ran off. Or was it the time before that?

The call came from someone at the power plant. Vicky's father had handed the phone to her and retreated to the basement, where he spent his days carving hunting decoys for trips he'd never take and drinking. The caller broke the news about Nana as gently as possible, but she also made it clear that they had a week to clean out the house before it was torn down.

Vicky knew that if she and Burt didn't handle it, no one would. They piled into Burt's wreck of a Mustang—no air conditioning and a staticky radio—for the eight-hour drive to Ohio, arriving at Cheshire Baptist Church just in time for the funeral, which had been arranged by what remained of the community.

Though Vicky received Christmas cards from Nana and phone calls on her birthdays, she hadn't been to Cheshire in over a decade. Not since the company that owned the power plant bought the town, lock, stock and barrel. Vicky vaguely remembers a small but thriving community. Now it's little more than a cluster of buildings—the church, an old brick post office, Town Hall, and a few businesses—near the only stoplight, and a handful of houses occupied by old timers who refused to leave. Even most of the streets are gone.

"No, I guess not," she says after a long pause. "I'll make more popcorn." They missed lunch and she isn't eager to go back to Triple B's Pizza, the only restaurant in town, frequented mostly by plant workers. She doesn't like the way the men ogle her. Burt says it's because of the way she dresses.

Burt opens the flap and dumps a small reel into his hand. They've been watching home movies for the past hour, ever since they found the box containing a projector and nearly a dozen boxes of 8mm film. Burt was initially stymied by the threading mechanism, but Vicky found the instructions on the Internet. He didn't like taking orders from her, but it was either that or fool around with the projector until he got frustrated and gave up.

Every now and then they recognize someone in the movies projected onto a sheet they tacked to the wall. Nana, their mother, their parents in happier times. Once they saw themselves as little children playing in the back yard. There were houses next door and picket fences, all gone now.

Once the popcorn is ready, Burt engages the projector motor and, when it's running smoothly, turns on the lamp. The instructions were very specific about this: the film might melt if it isn't moving when the lamp is on. The shaky image shows a river, probably the Ohio. The camera zooms in on the wreckage of a bridge deck dangling from a support pier into the water.

"Omigosh," Vicky says. "Look at that."

"I remember hearing about this," Burt says. "Back in the sixties. The Silver Bridge—that's it. A bunch of people died."

The camera pans from left to right, revealing the destruction at both ends. Most of the bridge has simply disappeared. "What is that?" Vicky asks, pointing at the rubble on one of the banks.

"It's a car."

"Jeez. Can you imagine? Having the world suddenly fall out from under you?" She shakes her head. "Wait. What was that?"

"Where?"

"It's gone—but . . . I'm not sure. Rewind it."

"What for?"

"You'd never believe me. You have to see it for yourself."

"There's no rewind," Burt says. He has that tone in his voice, the one that says she's trying his patience. "We have to wait until the end."

"Can't you release the clutch and rewind it by hand?"

In the flickering light, she sees the annoyed look Burt gives her. He usually contradicts anything she says automatically. Now, though, he surprises her. He grudgingly nods and says, "Maybe."

He switches off the lamp and disengages the clutch. The twin reels stop. He grasps the front one and pulls film from the take-up reel. "Far enough?" he asks. When Vicky nods—though she has no idea, to be honest—he re-engages the clutch and flips the projector lamp back on.

"Come here," Vicky says, waving him closer to the screen.

The scene repeats. The shaky camera pans from one end of the collapsed bridge to the other. The lens zooms in to reveal the damaged car among the piles of twisted metal.

"There!" Vicky says, poking her finger at the sheet, making it ripple.

"What? That?" A second later, the camera pans away. "Just some guy."

"He has wings," Vicky says.

"What? That's crazy."

"Look at it again. I swear."

They watch the brief scene five more times. The figure standing stationary among the remains of the ruined bridge does indeed appear to have huge, gossamer wings. It also has no head, but has what look like enormous eyes near its shoulders.

Finally, they let the movie run through to the end, but the creature never shows up, again. When the last of the film threads through the sprockets, Burt shuts the machine down. "Do you know what that was?"

Vicky shakes her head in the now-dark room.

"This is huge. Better than that blurry footage of Bigfoot."

"What are you talking about?"

"Mothman," Burt says.

"Who's that? Some superhero?" Burt is addicted to graphic novels, though he can ill afford them.

"No, he's real. They made a movie about him. With that old dude, you know, from the film with Julia Roberts about the hooker."

Vicky blinks when he turns on the pole lamp. She shakes her head and shrugs.

"Don't you remember? Grandpa talked about Mothman all the time. There were lots of sightings down in Point Pleasant. This is like having footage of Sasquatch. Inside Area 51."

"You're a goofball."

"I'm serious." He shows her articles on his phone, some from legitimate newspapers.

Vicky has to agree that what they saw resembles the descriptions in various accounts from over the years. "Maybe it's a statue," she says.

"Hardly." Burt snorts. "The first sighting was barely a year before the bridge collapsed. They did put one up in Point Pleasant, but that was only a few years ago."

Vicky can't shake the mental image of that eerie creature lurking among the wreckage. Forty-six people died, according to the articles. In freezing water.

"Some people think Mothman was trying to warn about the bridge," Burt says.

"Didn't do a very good job, did he?"

He ignores this. "Others think a sonic boom from his wings caused it."

When Vicky giggles, Burt's eyebrows furrow. "It's true." He removes the film from the projector and places it carefully into its box.

"But we've got him."

"What do we do with it?"

"I don't know. Maybe CNN will buy it. Or that show on SyFy about the ghost hunters."

Vicky looks at all the boxes they still have to go through. When they started, they'd joked about discovering treasure. Stacks of cash or gold bars. So far, they found one twenty-dollar bill jutting from the pages of a magazine, and some old jewelry and figurines that might be worth a couple of hundred bucks total, according to eBay. With what they hope to bring in at the yard sale, they'll barely have enough to cover food and gas for the trip.

"Let's get back to work," she says.

"Why bother?" Burt says. "We're gonna be famous."

"We might find something else," Vicky says. Her brother is three years older and can usually browbeat her into doing things, but her approach with him is subtler. "Another film, maybe."

Burt's eyes widen. He tears open boxes with renewed enthusiasm and by the end of the afternoon they've gone through everything in the living room. They find a few more items that might have some re-sale value, and Burt yelps when he turns up an envelope containing sixty-five dollars in old bills. Nothing relating to Mothman, though.

They use the cash to treat themselves to dinner at Bennigan's in Point Pleasant, passing the power station along the way. While they eat, Burt can't stop talking about Mothman and how valuable the film is. Before returning to Cheshire, he makes a detour to see the statue, a 12-foot behemoth in the downtown area that only vaguely resembles the creature they saw on the film.

"Maybe they'd know what to do with it," Vicky says, pointing at the nearby Mothman Museum (and Gift Shop), which has already closed for the day.

"They'd want us to give it to them," Burt says. "Or they'd make copies when we weren't looking."

Her brother inherited his mistrust of anything official from their father, who often turns crimson and shakes his fist at the screen while watching the evening news, muttering about the cheats and liars in Washington. She doesn't know how Burt is ever going to trust anyone with the film, but for now she remains silent. She'll have to do her own research. If the film clip is valuable—which she still doubts—she figures she can find the best way to capitalize on it.

Vicky wakes up in a dark room, disoriented. After a few seconds she remembers where she is: in the bed her grandparents occupied for decades, where Nana slept alone after Grandpa died.

The vivid dream that woke her dissipates. She blinks and looks toward the window. What she sees makes her catch her breath: a pair of luminous red dots. Mothman has glowing red eyes, according to the stories she read. Until yesterday she would never have given such a thing a second thought, but there's no way Grandpa could have faked that footage—not with that old camera. They have absolute proof of a mythological creature.

Maybe it knows. Maybe it's coming after them to destroy the film.

She slides from bed, the wood floor rough under her bare feet as she approaches the window at an angle and looks out into the night. The glowing embers multiply. Some are yellow. They flicker and flash. It's the power plant at the south edge of Cheshire. It doesn't seem right that a place that spews enough poison to kill a town should look so pretty, lit up like a Christmas tree.

Grandpa used to complain about how the plant was supposed to bring jobs to the area when it was built in the 1950s but few local people had been employed there. Its twin stacks and the shorter cooling chimneys are visible from everywhere in town. Their output usually appears to be harmless white steam, but it's laced with toxic bands of grey and yellow.

When it turns blue, everyone knows to stay indoors. The locals call it the blue plume, and it can be thick enough to make drivers turn on their headlights in the daytime. The scrubbers the company installed at great expense unexpectedly converted the sulfur from the local coal into an acid aerosol that causes headaches, eye irritation, asthma, and burns on lips and tongues. It peels the paint from the walls of houses and kills birds.

When people complained, the company decided it was cheaper to buy the town and make everyone move than clean up the plant, according to the Widow's Club, a weekly gathering of Cheshire's remaining residents, down to five now that Nana's gone. Vicky joined them for supper after the funeral and heard the whole story. Burt had no interest in old people's reminiscences so he went on to the house.

Nana was deeply disappointed in her former neighbors, the women said. They took the money and ran, even though most moved only a few miles down the road. Americans are supposed to stand up for what they believe in and fight corporate greed, one feisty octogenarian said—the one who boasted that she'd buried three husbands. It sounded like an oft-discussed subject. Her father would probably agree.

Standing near the window, looking out into the night, Vicky feels vulnerable. She can't shake the sense of being watched. If the creature is as powerful as they say, what might he do to prevent being exposed? She shouldn't have read those articles before going to bed. She imagines Mothman lurking out there, waiting for the right moment to flap his enormous wings, causing a sonic boom that will level Nana's house the way he destroyed the Silver Bridge.

Vicky feels her way back to bed in the unfamiliar room. She lies awake, staring into the darkness. Mothman is visible on the film for no more than two seconds, twenty or thirty frames at most, but Burt says each one is worth its weight in gold. What might people do when presented with incontrovertible evidence of the existence of a legendary supernatural creature?

Vicky thinks about glowing red eyes and flashing lights.

Burt can hardly contain his excitement the next morning as they eat cold cereal from the pantry with milk from the Cheshire Food Mart. "I had a great idea," he says. "Instead of finding a place to copy the film, why not just film it?"

"Huh?"

"Use my phone to record the movie off the screen."

"People will think you faked it," Vicky says.

"We have the original. That's no fake."

No, it isn't, she thinks. There's no denying the original. "We still have a lot of work to do here. The yard sale's tomorrow."

"Forget that," Burt says. "Chump change." Once he latches onto something, it's impossible to change his mind. He's the most obstinate person she's ever known, besides their father.

"Okay," she says. The look of surprise on Burt's face is rewarding. He expected her to put up a fight. "I'll clean up the dishes. You get the projector ready."

"Why bother? In a few days, this place will be history."

"It's just something I have to do," she says.

Burt is too excited to argue. While she runs water into the dishpan, she hears him muttering as he threads the film through the sprockets. She stares out the window over the sink at the vacant landscape where a town once existed. In a heartbeat, everything changed. A blue plume appeared, the company handed out stacks of money and almost everyone abandoned Cheshire.

What would a stack of money do to Burt? To her?

She leaves the dishes to drain on the sideboard and heads toward the living room. She hears the distinctive clack-clack-click of the film running through the projector. She sees Burt's shadow on the wall as he stands off to one side, waiting to record the image being projected onto the sheet.

So much destruction, so much death, she thinks as she takes in the wreckage of the Silver Bridge. People are always looking for reasons why things like this happen. A defective eyebar, according to news articles. A sonic boom caused by Mothman's flapping wings, according to less authoritative reports.

Burt has his arm extended, ready to capture the historic frames on his phone. The only footage of a myth in existence. The proof that will change everything.

Vicky glides toward the projector. She knows where the switch is from the instructions she read to Burt. Moving with deliberate purpose, she disengages the clutch. The film stops at the beginning of Mothman's brief but monumental appearance.

"Hey, that's good," Burt says. In his excitement, he's forgotten about the warnings. A second later, he shrieks. "What? What's happening? Oh, no. No! No! No!"

He pushes her aside and fumbles with switches, but it's too late. The static image on the screen is melting and twisting under the intense heat of the projector bulb. The smell of burnt plastic fills the room.

When Vicky turns on the floor lamp, prepared to put on the best acting performance of her life—*I had no idea, Burt, honest. I was just trying to help!*—she sees a puff of smoke rising from the projector. *A blue plume,* she thinks, *the end of someone else's dreams.*

De Moffman Comeff

By S. Clayton Rhodes

> It has been argued that the Mothman may originate not from some distant star but from some dimension parallel to our own, and that he may only be biding his time before paying another visit to our world, if in fact he ever existed at all.
>
> — Dr. Hans Richter, Author of *A Paranormal Handbook*

The life of a single mother was never easy, but a single mother of a child with a disability had an even tougher row to hoe. Ginger Farnham knew this all too well, but she never shirked her duties as a parent. If anything, her son's disability only strengthened her resolve to be the best mother she could be.

Heading west out of Point Pleasant, Ginger pulled her vehicle onto the crushed gravel lot of Wee Care Daycare. The sky was the color of slate and hung heavy with the promise of rain as she went inside. Davy's teacher, Miss Pritchard, had wanted to talk to Ginger about Davy's recent behavior, and though she'd insisted it was nothing serious, Ginger had promised to take her lunch break early and come down to speak with her immediately.

Just past a cork bulletin board displaying snapshots from the class's last birthday party, Ginger rapped at the glass panel of the door to room three. The children were in a circle doing a flash-card activity and calling out letters of the alphabet. Miss Pritchard left the class under the care of her aide.

"Thanks so much for coming, Ms. Farnham," she said, closing the door behind her. "Really, it could have waited until this evening when you came to get him. I just wanted to alert you ahead of time that we should talk—"

Ginger waved it off. "That's all right. What's the trouble?"

"Well, as I said on the phone, it's really not *trouble*. Well, maybe it would be easier to just show you."

Miss Pritchard led her to a small, dim office down the hall where she opened a metal filing cabinet and pulled out several thick squares of manila drawing paper. She spread them out onto a worktable for Ginger to see. On each page was a colorful drawing of a butterfly; some were done in markers, some in crayon, and more still were a combination of both. Ginger would've recognized the drawing style as Davy's, even if his name hadn't been printed in haphazard letters in the upper right hand corners.

She raised an eyebrow. "Okay. So he's making pictures of butterflies?"

Miss Pritchard looked distinctly uncomfortable, as if trying to decide how best to broach the next part. "Not butterflies. They're supposed to be the Mothman. According to Davy."

Looking closer, Ginger *could* make out human bodies at the center of the wings, and apart from the insect eyes and beak-like mouths, the heads looked pretty much man-like.

"How long has this been going on?"

"Since Tuesday. I didn't tell you immediately because I thought it was something he would just move on from. But now it seems he's fixated. All morning he's separated himself from the other children. He won't interact, won't speak, and when I encouraged him to put away the art supplies and join us on the mats for a game, he started slapping himself."

Ginger's brow furrowed. "That's not like him. Would it be all right if I spoke to him?"

In the classroom, Ginger knelt beside Davy. He hardly bothered to look up from his work: cutting wings with safety scissors. His tongue poked past his chapped lips in concentration, and Ginger could see the heels of both his hands were blotchy from Crayola marker ink.

Davy had been born with Down's Syndrome four years ago, and his father had skipped out shortly thereafter, saying he didn't want anything to do with "any Mongoloid baby," to which Ginger had thought, *Good riddance. You'd just be in the way, anyway.* John Farnham had been a shiftless man who worked only when he felt like it—which was seldom at best—and spent the rest of his time watching ballgames from the recliner, swilling beer, and complaining about how little there was in their bank account. Ginger was never so glad as when he left. It saved her the trouble of kicking him out.

It had been an uphill struggle trying to raise Davy on her own, but better to go it alone than with an unwilling partner. Despite all the challenges, though, Ginger was adamant Davy should have the same opportunities as every other child. This also meant a commitment from Davy to socialize with other children and do his best to fit in—which wasn't exactly happening at the moment.

"Davy." She gently lifted his chin. "Davy, please look at me."

Reluctant to stop his current project, he peered up at her with wide, almond eyes.

"Now, why don't you tell me what this is about? Miss Pritchard says you were slapping yourself earlier. Is that true?"

He gave a small shrug and frowned. "I wanted to work on my pictures."

"What is it that you've been drawing, Davy?" He had a small stack of drawings, cutouts, and collages beside him. Swirls of dried Elmer's glue decorated some of the construction paper.

"De Moffman, Mama." He always did have trouble with his "th" sounds. "De Moffman's comin'."

His bland expression seemed to suggest this was something Ginger should already know. She couldn't fathom why the sudden fixation with the Mothman, though. Sure, he'd been to the festival, and they passed the life-sized statue downtown half a dozen times any given week, but she doubted he understood the significance of what the Mothman was. Not that she did herself; celebrating a mythical figure supposedly seen by only a handful of people in the late sixties always seemed rather silly to her.

"He *is*, Mama. De Moffman's comin'. Dat's what he tole me."

"All right, Davy. If you say so."

She kissed his forehead, said to keep up the good work, then out of hearing range from him, she advised Miss Pritchard they should let things run their course for the time being.

After finishing out her work day, Ginger returned to pick Davy up at quarter past five and stopped off at the grocery story for dinner: rotisserie chicken from the deli, mashed potatoes and rolls—one of Davy's favorite meals.

In the checkout lane, though, something happened that made Ginger wonder if she'd been wrong in not taking what was going on at the daycare more seriously. She looked away from Davy for a second—it couldn't have been longer than that—and in that time, he had removed one of the magazines from the wire display rack, opened it up, removed a page from the center, and proceeded to fold it into the rough shape of a moth. Ginger was in time only to catch him bending the last wing into place.

"Look, Mama," he said, holding up the impromptu piece of origami. "It's de Moffman."

He smiled broadly, seeing nothing wrong in ruining one of the store magazines. Ginger took it and asked him not to do it again.

"You'll have to pay for that," the girl beyond the conveyor belt said. The customer ahead of them had just left and they were next.

"I'm sorry. Of course, I'll pay for it," Ginger said. "He just didn't know what he was doing."

"Yeah, well, you still hafta pay for it." The girl, who couldn't have been more than seventeen and who never stopped cracking her wad of blue gum, apparently hadn't heard Ginger. "Parents gotta *watch* their kids in here." Then a puzzled look crossed her face. "What's the matter with your boy, anyway? He got something wrong with him?"

Ginger ached to say, *"Are you blind? Can't you see he has a disability?"* but in the end she held her tongue. She was already used to the looks strangers gave Davy whenever they were in public, everything from sly glances to full-on stares. But very seldom was anyone so insensitive that they came right out and said something.

"No, there's nothing wrong with him." She placed her items onto the conveyor belt while avoiding eye contact with the cashier. "Not a thing in the world."

Nothing except for his apparent obsession with the Mothman.

What bothered her most was that normally Davy's fingers weren't particularly nimble. He took great care and time when doing anything very involved. So how had he been able to fold up that paper so quickly?

27

Following supper, Davy asked to be excused, but instead of turning on the TV, per his usual routine, he retreated to his room while Ginger finished washing the dinner dishes.

Once the dishes were dried and put away, Ginger went to check on him. There on his nightstand was a two-foot-tall sculpture of the Mothman, formed of multi-colored Play-Doh pressed together over a framework of pencils, which jutted out in various places. Wings made from cardboard and bits of tissue paper stuck out in back of the crouching figure. It was actually a good likeness, if a little disturbing. The beaked face seemed to look up at Ginger with its clear marble eyes.

She hadn't noticed the half dozen other drawings Scotch-taped to Davy's wall, either.

"When did you do these?" she asked.

"Dis mornin', when you were takin' your shower."

Ginger nodded and took a seat on the edge of Davy's bed, absently smoothing the *Toy Story* bedspread as she spoke. "Honey, I'd like to know why you're so interested in the Mothman all of a sudden. Has someone been talking to you about him or—"

"He visits me, Mama. At night mostly. And he says stuff to me sometimes."

"And what sort of things does the Mothman say?"

"He says he's comin' back soon."

Ginger rubbed her arms at the sudden draft she knew she'd only just imagined. This was not the first time Davy had spoken of seeing things in dreams, and often the dreams proved to have great significance.

Six months ago, he had told her of the dream in which his grandmother was hurt by a big, long gray dog with wheels. Long gray dog with wheels! It sounded like such a funny image, just the sort of thing a child would imagine, and yet the following day Ginger received word that her mother, while driving to the post office in Cumberland, Maryland, had been hit by a Greyhound bus with shoddy brakes and was in intensive care.

Greyhound bus: "long gray dog with wheels." Considering he was a young boy with Down's, his prediction didn't seem that far off. Another time, he'd dreamt of Ginger getting a check for "a lotta money." A week later, she was promoted to head of her department at the Career Center when her supervisor unexpectedly turned in his resignation.

The Mothman, however, was something else altogether. He was something made up, an urban legend, which had grown through word of mouth for so long, the locals believed it to be real.

"Does he say anything else, honey?"

Davy's gaze drifted ceilingward in recollection. "He says I am a . . . I don't remember the word, but it was like a door."

Ginger said, "A gate?"

Davy pointed a chubby index finger at her. Pink Play-Doh underscored its nail. "Dat's it! A gate. I knew it was someffin' you walk frough."

Ginger stood, ruffled his hair, and told him if he washed his hands and put on his PJs, he could have an hour of TV before bedtime. Davy was finally able to let go of his artwork. Ginger supposed it had something to do with his being able to express what he had on his mind. Maybe that was what he needed all along.

That night, after she'd been asleep for maybe an hour, Davy came into her room. He was a dim, dark figure, black against the rest of the blackness surrounding him, but she could make out his outline.

"What is it, sweetie? Another dream or do you need a drink?"

"No, Mama." Davy shook his head. "I wanted to tell you . . ."

"Tell me what, honey?"

"Dat it's almos' time."

"Time? Time for what?"

He toyed with the hem of his pajama top. "For de Moffman to come back."

From out of the darkness behind him, a face formed, as well as a torso, shimmering chrome-bright in the gloom. But the features were of nothing human.

A scream stuck somewhere before it reached Ginger's lips as she took in the toothed beak and iridescent eyes. Huge wings unfurled behind the body with a sound like canvas tarps snapping in a chill, damp breeze.

This was the statue of the Mothman from town, only somehow it had become animate. Steel had morphed into mobile flesh, and now its taloned hands glinted in the half-light, its fingers as long and pointed as the tines of a pitchfork. Worse yet, these claws rested on Davy's shoulders . . . so dangerously sharp, so dangerously close to his head!

"I'm his gate, Mama. But don't worry," Davy said. "He says it will be quick."

Ginger wanted to cry out, "Don't hurt my son! Don't hurt him, *please*!" but again her voice locked up, her tongue thick and frozen behind her teeth.

Then Davy was raising his pajama top, as if ready to show her a spot where his belly hurt. But there was no stomach there! Only a gaping rectangle of purest white light—light so bright it threatened to sear

Ginger's eyes—and before she could do anything she was swept up off her feet and went tumbling into that brightness. The top and sides of the opening swelled, lengthened and expanded as wind whipped her hair wildly about her face, and she went tumbling, tumbling, flailing wildly into the void.

Ginger screamed herself awake. It had been a dream, after all. But her pulse still thrummed, and she realized she had a splitting headache. Fumbling in the drawer of her nightstand, she found and managed to work the cap off a bottle of Advil. She shook out two caplets, dry-swallowing them while heading for the kitchen for some water to chase them with.

There at the sink, with the water still running, she glanced out the small window.

The glass dropped from her nerveless hand and into the basin, shattering to bits.

She pushed aside the sheer to get a better view and make sure she was really seeing what she thought she was seeing.

It was true. On the back lawn, perhaps only thirty feet from the house, stood . . . well, she couldn't even begin to count how many deer, neighborhood cats, squirrels, rabbits, raccoons, possums. Here was the vague outline of an owl, there a red fox, appearing silver in the wash of harvest moonlight. One figure might have been that of a stray dog or even a coyote. All the animals stood side by side, oblivious to the fact that some were natural enemies. They made no noise whatsoever, and stranger still . . . each had its head bowed low to the ground. It was as if they all had some single, reverent purpose.

The time on the microwave—3:36—barely registered with Ginger as she ran to another window. Through the living room, she saw more wildlife lined up in the same way. This time they stretched across a vacant field on the far side of the street, at approximately the same distance from the house as the animals in back. The small window in the bathroom faced the McGill's, and when she went in and peered past the blinds she could see the outlines of birds on their roof. All the animals and birds seem to form a perfect ring around the house.

Ginger had no idea what it all meant, but she was sure it had something do with Davy's prophecy that the Mothman was coming soon.

In the upper drawer of her bureau, buried beneath her socks, she kept a .22 pistol for the purpose of home defense. She'd even learned to shoot it on a firing range with pretty fair accuracy. Just in case any of the coyotes or dogs out there turned out to be rabid and decided to launch through a window, she dug out the pistol and inserted the clip. Keeping the safety on, she slid it under her pillow for easy access, then she went and scooped up Davy and brought him to sleep in her room so she could watch over him.

Davy's head jerked back and forth as she carried him, but he didn't wake up.

Eventually, after a couple more hours of restlessness, she was able to get back to sleep herself.

The next morning, while Davy was getting dressed, Ginger walked outside with her mug of instant Sanka. All the animals were gone, of course, but she did find places where the grass had become matted down from their passing. Additionally, there were deer hoof prints and various droppings, but that was all. Whatever had brought the animals here had likewise sent them on their way at some point before dawn.

Ginger knew Down's Syndrome was caused by extra genetic material being passed on to a person through their twenty-first chromosome. In light of Davy's sometimes uncanny predictions, she wondered if this extra genetic material might account for his strange ability. Could it be Davy had been given a special gift to offset his disability?

She didn't know, but that explanation felt right. It would not, however, explain that business with the animals.

Once Davy was finished with his bowl of Froot Loops, they climbed into her Datsun, heading for the daycare. It was cold, even for an October morning, and she had to kick on the car's defrost to clear away the opaque fog covering the windshield.

"Davy," she said, "all that talk about the Mothman, and the artwork . . . . Are you finished with that now?" He hadn't made any more drawings or sculptures since last evening.

She could see him through the rearview mirror, shaking his head. "No, Mama. De Moffman *is* comin'. He really is!"

Ginger caught a glimpse of something large overhead as she drove. They were facing into the sun, though, so it was hard to see, but a silhouette resembling that of a large bird was clear in the sky approaching them, and she was certain if the ratcheting heater had been switched off, she would have heard a noise like canvas tarps flapping in the wind.

No, Davy, she thought. *For once you're wrong. The Mothman isn't coming. He's already here . . .*

Eli and the Bridge

By Karin Fuller

Sanders slapped Eli on the back, nearly clipping his wing. "What do you know? It finally happened."

Eli smiled broadly, holding his three matching cards in the air for all at the table to see.

"Told you if you waited long enough, it was bound to happen," Ren said. Over the years, Ren had been the most supportive of Eli's desire for the big do-over, his wish to make things right.

"Talk about your long shots," Sanders said. "Figured the best you'd draw is another flood."

Eli waggled his cards at Sanders to rub it in just a bit, and then laid the cards on the table in order, side by side, edges touching. When he'd drawn the first card back in 1972, just five years after the Silver Bridge collapse, most everyone urged him to draw again—even Sanders, who generally behaved as though the field of competitors was only Eli and him. But Eli understood odds, knew nothing fair or rational determined what anyone drew. It was luck, plain and simple.

For years, he'd held that first card, the one showing the left side of a bridge, and in 1982, had drawn the second, showing the right. Choosing to hold was easier then. It still limited his possibilities for other sets, since he'd need to draw to the inside, the center of the bridge, and they could only draw or hold five.

Bridges were Eli's obsession. No other disasters were nearly as satisfying, or as potentially redeeming. He'd draw to the inside, and this would be the do-over to end all do-overs.

Eli had been so close to goal with the Silver Bridge that his failure had made him something of a legend among the players. His planning, patience and near-perfect execution had prevented him from being openly mocked, but his dogged determination for a do-over made some of the younger ones, like Sanders, view Eli as pitiable. Gone was the adoration he'd attained through his prowess on previous levels.

Back in '67, Eli had been cocky. He'd been excited, overeager. Sloppy. But he'd also been lucky.

Rush hour traffic. Icy cold December waters. Forty-six deaths.

He'd somehow plucked the perfect eyebar. That, he'd done right. The straw that broke the camel's back had been No. 330.

Bridges were built different these days. Engineered better. Inspected better. Yet they all still had a weak spot, if you knew where to look.

Eli knew.

Of all the cards in the deck, Eli believed the bridge cards had the most potential, though only if one could be patient. It could take months to find the right bridge, to sniff out its weakness, to establish a plan of action and determine just the right time. Hardest for Eli would come after finding the flaw—being able to resist the temptation to test the weak spot with just a little tug, certain he could resist tugging too hard.

If he could do that, there was no reason he couldn't win the whole enchilada, even in a state as small as West Virginia.

Back in '83, Zegeer had completed a bridge set. He'd been so excited he'd gone straight to the Mianus River Bridge in Greenwich, Connecticut. He'd quickly spotted a weakness in the pin-and-hanger assembly and simply couldn't help himself. It was middle of the night in June, traffic practically nonexistent: Zegeer had been lucky to get three points.

Mosby had completed the most recent set. His choice had such potential—a bridge in Minnesota, one of the coldest states in the nation. Could've wreaked total havoc. Racked up serious points. But after finding the flaw, Archie just had to give it a tug. He'd been lucky it was rush hour. He collected 13.

These were the cautionary tales Eli kept in the front of his mind.

When Eli had drawn his first complete set back in 1967, he'd quickly chosen his target. West Virginia had many bridges, and at that time, most were poorly maintained. The potential in the Silver Bridge had been easy to see. He just needed to bide time until the weather and traffic conditions were ideal.

Eli had been holing up at an abandoned TNT factory for months, but boredom caused him to get careless and be seen. Two couples in a car managed to get far too good a look at him, and they'd chased him for miles after he'd gathered himself enough to take flight.

The next night, while searching for a new place to stay, he was spotted by two more humans. A week later, it happened again, then again. He was hardly surprised when he felt himself being spotted the day he went to the bridge, but he was so determined by then—had mentally calculated how many he'd need just to break even—that nothing was going to stop him from getting that number.

And he had. Plus a few more.

Just not enough.

"So do you have a location in mind?" Ren asked when the annual card drawing had ended.

Eli shrugged, smoothing one wing with the tip of the other. Most everyone had finished their drinks, saying goodbyes.

"Not really," Eli said, his mind ticking with possibilities. The Nitro-

St. Albans Bridge would be almost too easy. That one-legged old lady had been tottering on the balance beam so long it would almost be a kindness to give her a shove. There was the Ices Ferry Bridge over Cheat Lake in Morgantown, with so many soft spots that Eli'd lost count. A poorly placed flock of pigeons could bring that puppy down.

"Can't interest you in trading for a plane crash, can I?" Sanders waggled his two cards. "Just a single engine Cessna, but in the hands of someone with mad skills like you. . ."

"Dream on," Zegeer said, drawing close enough to get between Eli and Sanders, just in case. "You'd need to be holding the Hoover Dam to get him to swap."

Eli smiled, nodded. The tension between him and Sanders was new. Theirs had been a good-natured one-upmanship, but seemed to be edging toward something darker.

"Later," Eli said, clapping a hand on Sanders's shoulder. Maybe squeezing a little too hard. "See you on the next level."

Eli climbed the stairs to the top of the old water tower, then climbed on top of the rail and leaned forward, his wings slightly open.

From this moment until his task was complete, Eli needed to keep reminding himself that he was now visible to humans. It was part of the game. His greatest challenge came from being so much larger than the others. He was easily a full head taller, probably 50 pounds heavier. Such bulk drew attention. The others could generally travel with storks or geese—especially that puny Sanders—and seldom be noticed, but along with his size, Eli's massive wings made a *whoosh* when he flew. He was forced to fly higher, to wait for the cover of storms and moonless nights to travel.

He spread his wings wide and then jumped.

Eli wanted his next splash to be big. *Legendary* big. The kind movies would be made about, much like his last. Except this time, there'd be no mention of sightings. All those Silver Bridge sightings had cost Eli most of his points the last time. That wouldn't happen again. For weeks, he'd been hiding in the woods overlooking the Interstate, biding his time.

Eli knew what his target would be. He'd been watching its construction for years. The new eastbound I-64 bridge between Institute and South Charleston was a cantilevered construction, supported only on the ends. There were no piers or structures beneath to hold up the weight of the middle, which involved eight seemingly unsupported spans, with a total length of 2,950 feet. The main span of 760 feet made it the longest concrete box girder span in the United States.

Many marveled that there could be such a long distance with no piers supporting the weight. Engineers insisted it was totally safe.

They'd said the same of the Titanic.

The Titanic would've been Ren's highest score ever—maybe *the* biggest score ever—except there had been sightings then, too. That most of those who'd sighted him ended up dying in the icy water didn't matter. Sightings were sloppy. They cost.

Eli wished expense could be considered as a factor in scoring. The price tag for this oddly engineered creation was $93.6 million.

That it was nearing completion just as he'd completed his set seemed like fate.

Eli wanted badly to fly, to soar above and then swoop down beneath his target, to see and feel it from all angles. To find its soft spot. Its fatal flaw.

But the night was too clear to risk flying, so he sat on a rock in his scooped-out edge of the woods, overlooking the bridge. The wind was stirring honeysuckle with lawn clippings and a coming rain, a scent so comforting that Eli had nearly drifted off to sleep when a sudden small gust from behind made him jump.

"Hi-diddly-do, neighbor," Sanders said. He folded his wings and crouched into the same arms-wrapped-around-knees position as Eli. "I wondered if this might be your chosen. It would've been mine, if I could've convinced you to trade. Lousy single-engine Cessna."

Eli chuckled, surprised to find himself glad for the company, especially considering the company was Sanders's.

"Put your mind to it," Eli said. "Could do a lot with a Cessna."

"Like what?"

"What about an air show?" Eli said. "Or a plane dragging a banner over a stadium during a game. You need to determine your target, and then be ready to strike when the time is right. Watch for the opportunity and then make your move."

Sanders tilted his head to the side, like a pup that's heard an odd sound. Eli couldn't help himself—he smiled.

"You just need to be patient," Eli said. "You have to wait until the moment is absolutely right, until the maximum number of points are in their most vulnerable state."

"I'm not so good at being patient," Sanders said.

"It's not our nature to be."

They sat in affable silence for a time, something that pleased Eli greatly. He'd not been one to enjoy companionship for many years. He seemed more suited for solitude.

"Care for a sip?" Sanders said, touching the tin to Eli's arm.

"Nectar?"

"Home grown," Sanders said. "Like drinking fast air."

Eli took a small sip, then another. His nostrils flared.

Sanders laughed.

The more nectar they downed, the easier talking became for the two former archrivals, who weren't really rivals at all. Sanders might've fancied himself Eli's equal, but luck was all that kept them playing on the same level—Sanders' good luck, Eli's bad.

"Gone dry," Eli said, tipping the tin upside down over his open mouth.

"Makes you crave the real thing, doesn't it?" Sanders said, looking up at the sky. They were nearly two hours into a new day. Traffic on the bridge had become almost nonexistent.

"Makes my wings itch," Eli said. He wiggled his shoulders and hugged tight his knees, as if to keep himself from standing and opening them full.

"How close are you to being ready?" Sanders gestured toward the bridge down the hill from where they sat.

"There's something I need that I'm not sure where to get," he said. "That green stuff they worship—the paper." He held up both hands, bending his fingers into the shape of a rectangle.

"You mean money?"

"That's it," said Eli. "I need much money. Bags of it."

"Easy, there's this place people have. You can get anything there. *Anything.*"

"You forgetting about these?" Eli wobbled his massive wings back and forth. "Did all that nectar make you forget we're visible to humans?"

Sanders grinned. "That's the best thing. This place attracts creatures far stranger than us. We could march all through there and still blend right in with the rest of the flock."

Eli and Sanders returned from Walmart with a bag of cash each.

The store hadn't been crowded, and those who were staggering up and down the aisles at 3 ᴬᴹ had seemed somehow damaged, with eyes that were glazed or flat or mostly dead.

They'd had some trouble finding where the money was kept, as it wasn't on the shelves but rather stored in the back, behind a thick door Eli had almost not been strong enough to open.

"Going to let me in on how this will help you bring down the bridge?" Sanders asked after they'd landed again in the hillside nook that Eli called home.

"Can't."

"You don't really believe in luck, do you?" Sanders said.

Eli shrugged.

Sanders kept after him, nagging and needling, going from agitated to angry to furious over Eli's refusal to give up anything beyond a single word: bait.

"I should've never helped you," Sanders said. He spat on the bag of money by Eli's feet, and then took to the sky.

It was time.

After so many years of construction, Eli expected there would be some sort of celebration—a ribbon-cutting or something—when the new bridge was finally opened to traffic, but it had been anticlimatic. The barriers were simply removed and cars and trucks began using the bridge.

Most of the bridge, anyway. One lane was still closed while signs were erected overhead and lighting installed. A bucket truck was parked on the bridge below one of those signs, which was still covered by a protective canvas tarp.

Eli'd had to work quickly to empty the money into the tarp without being seen, but he'd been watching long enough that he knew the best times. A few bills had flown loose, caught the breeze. But there were plenty more.

When finished, he flew underneath the bridge and checked his marks to make sure they'd survived the last rain. There were so many flaws to choose from. The vanity of those who'd designed this unsupported monstrosity amused Eli. They'd made it so simple for him. The hardest part had been devising how to get the most points, watching the traffic patterns, determining when to pull the cord to release the money. Doing so without being seen.

Eli had done his homework. What humans valued the greatest— what they most carefully guarded and protected—were what earned the most points. Humans in this part of the world valued their small ones the highest, and Eli had observed that the smalls were often moved from place to place on yellow buses. The wrinkled ones earned the least points, but Eli had found no way to discern what their modes of transportation might be.

The yellow buses began crossing the bridge intermittently at 7:47 AM, continuing until 8:15 AM.

Eli pulled the cord at 7:55.

The tarp dropped open and money rained down onto the passing traffic.

From below, where Eli was clinging to the bridge, he heard the squeal of brakes, heard the thud and crash of cars banging into one another, of car doors opening and yelling and laughter. The sound of feet. More feet. The higher-pitched voices of the smalls. Their squeals. Random words. Sounds of anger and amusement and greed. Voices raised.

So many voices.

Eli closed his eyes and forced himself to be patient, to allow as many as possible to gather.

It was time.

Moving with seemingly impossible speed, Eli hit one mark, then another.

The bridge lurched.

Cars slammed together. There was screaming. Commotion.

Eli hit his next two marks and the bridge shifted again, back the opposite direction.

A single small car flipped over the edge of the bridge. Eli saw it was empty.

A large chunk of the right pier broke loose and fell into the river, and with it, the exit ramp part of the bridge.

The middle dropped down, spilling more cars—empty ones—into the water. With each teetering of the bridge, there were more screams, but then it inexplicably stopped.

What remained was defying gravity. There was only a sliver of beam holding up the end. All it needed was a really hard—*something*—to make it snap.

Eli was trying frantically, using every ounce of his strength.

So close. So close.

He was almost there.

When he heard the sound of a single engine Cessna.

Heard Sanders call out, "Hi-diddly-do, neighbor!" in that last moment before the plane crashed into the bridge.

Secret of the Mothmen

By Brian J. Hatcher

Lawrence Treadway never thought he'd dread the success he'd worked so hard to earn. He knew the journey would be tough. There are no diplomas in this field. Experts are self-made, every one of them. Lawrence merely wanted a chance to prove himself, to receive even a modicum of respect, but it seemed no one would ever give him that chance.

Eventually, one of the smaller journals published an article Lawrence sent them. No pay, but it led to a second article, and a third. Slowly his publishing credits grew to a respectable body of work. Others began to take notice. Several conventions invited Lawrence to be a guest speaker. He did a few radio interviews. He even appeared on television once. And then, after his nonfiction book proposal collected a stack of rejections, Other Worlds Press said yes. A smaller publisher, sure, but Lawrence knew if he got his book out there, it would catch fire and become a success. At last, he thought, all his hard work was beginning to pay off.

But an email from Doug Keaton, Lawrence's editor, caused the bottom to drop out from under his dreams.

Ufology has its share of weirdos. No one denies that. But Lawrence Treadway had no intention in becoming one of them. He wasn't some crackpot who chased every sighting or crop circle that came his way. His job was to cut through all the hearsay and rumors with a dogged determination to get to the truth. And he was good. He reported several UFO sightings previously unknown to the general public. He disclosed documents that shed new light on the secret agendas still carried out at the infamous Hangar 18 in Area 51. He also uncovered an increase in Men in Black activity just prior to the events of 9/11. Lawrence had earned his reputation as a serious journalist the right way.

And now his editor was asking him to throw that reputation away.

On the surface, Mr. Keaton's request seemed a simple one. After all, weren't the stories out of Point Pleasant, West Virginia, as much a part of UFO lore as the Incan astronauts or the mysteries of Easter Island? Shouldn't a book about UFOs dedicate at least one chapter to the Mothman? Just to be comprehensive?

Lawrence wanted to squelch the Mothman chapter the minute Mr. Keaton mentioned it, but he didn't. It had been difficult finding a publisher interested in his book. Lawrence might not find another. But the idea was ridiculous. No serious ufologist cared about some winged beastie someone's Cousin Jed claimed to have seen after waking up in the back of a pickup. Lawrence built his reputation upon separating truth from fantasy. Giving space in his book to a bunch of backwoods tales could ruin his reputation and his career as an ufologist. But heaven forbid his book should fail to capitalize on the lucrative truck stop market.

Lawrence finally told Mr. Keaton he would need to do a little research on the Mothman for the new chapter. He took some time off from his day job in mid-September and booked a room at the Super 8 in Point Pleasant the week of the Mothman Festival.

It would be an 8-hour drive from Sandy Springs, Georgia, to Point Pleasant. Spend a week there, go to the festival on the weekend, drive home early the next week, and by then Lawrence might figure a way out of his predicament or at least come up with the chapter Mr. Keaton wanted but still minimize the damage to Lawrence's reputation.

Mr. Keaton suggested Lawrence could be a guest speaker at the Festival, but Lawrence talked him out of it. Keeping a low profile,

Lawrence said, would make it easier to get the interviews he needed. Truth was Lawrence didn't want to spend more time validating Mothman nonsense than he had to.

That's why he was surprised to find a message waiting for him when he checked into the Super 8.

"Who's it from?" Lawrence asked.

"I couldn't tell you," said the front desk clerk. "There's no name on the envelope, and I wasn't working this morning so I didn't see who dropped it off. Maybe it's from someone back home?"

"Maybe."

"Here's your key. Enjoy the festival."

"How did you know I was here for the festival?"

"That's why most of the people checking in this week are here. Also, I recognize your name. I've heard you on the radio. You here looking for the Mothman?"

"I'm here looking for the truth."

"You know what they say. The truth is out there."

"Yes," said Lawrence. "That's what they say."

Lawrence opened the envelope once he settled into his room. Inside, a card with a message handwritten in a strangely precise script. "You're looking for answers. I have those answers. I will stop by your room at 7:00 p.m. this evening." And the message was signed, God help us all, "Mr. X".

What the heck? thought Lawrence. One crackpot's as good as another. And he still had time to get a nap in. Lawrence figured he'd need it.

When Lawrence answered the door, a neat, nondescript gentleman stood waiting on the other side. "Hello, Mr. Treadway."

"You must be Mr. X."

"I most certainly must be."

"You're right on time," Lawrence said. "Almost exactly."

"Actually, your watch is three minutes fast. May I come in?"

"Of course." Lawrence gestured for Mr. X to enter and then closed the door behind them.

"Did I interrupt dinner?" Mr. X asked.

"Oh, you mean the Domino's box? No, just having a little snack."

"What did you order?"

"Large veggie. I like to pretend I'm eating healthy. Care for a slice?"

"No, thank you." Mr. X took a seat in the chair by the window and Lawrence sat down near him on the bed.

"So, do I call you 'Mr. X' or do you have another name you'd prefer?"

"Don't I wish. But you know how these things go. Maintaining an air of theatricality in situations such as ours is ever so important, wouldn't you say?"

"I suppose. So, you said you have answers for me."

"I do. Assuming you have questions."

"Let's start with an easy one. How did you know I was going to be here?"

"That is an easy one. Well, you know what they say about small towns."

"I do, actually," said Lawrence. "I grew up in Blairsville, Georgia. But I didn't stay. I guess I'm more of a big city kind of guy."

"As for myself, I can't really say I have a preference."

"Are you from around here?"

"Why do you ask?"

"You don't strike me as a native."

"You mean, I don't sound like an extra out of Disney's *Song of the South*."

"I'm sorry," Lawrence said. "I didn't mean to insult you."

"I'm not insulted. But others might be. And that could be detrimental during your interviews. Just a tip."

"I'll keep that in mind."

"Perception is everything," said Mr. X. "Oh, but I'm getting ahead of myself. What's your next question?"

"What do you know about the Mothman?"

"A great deal. I'm an expert on a number of things. But the Mothman isn't why you're here, is it?"

"If not for the Mothman, why would I be here?"

Mr. X smiled. "I sense a crafty bit of poetic truth hidden behind those words. But if you prefer the roundabout approach, we can talk about the Mothman if you like. I assume we can skip over the Wikipedia definition."

"Definitely."

"I don't know, it seems like an awful long drive just to gather a bit of local perspective on the Mothman. Especially if you're not sure how much truth there is in our local legend."

"That's what I'm here to find out."

"No, I don't think so. I think you've already made up your mind."

"Why do you say that?"

"Because I'm here to be interviewed and you haven't touched that tape recorder sitting on the night stand."

"You're right," Lawrence said. "Let me set up, and we'll talk."

"Don't worry about it. You won't need the recorder just now."

"You won't let me interview you about the Mothman?"

"We'll talk about the Mothman. More importantly, I'm also here to tell you the Truth."

"The truth about what?"

"How do I explain? Let's use this as an example. You've heard of H.P. Lovecraft?"

"The writer? Sure."

"As a child, he had nightmares about lanky creatures with huge wings. He'd later use them in his stories."

"Nightgaunts."

"Exactly. He also populated the Appalachian Mountains with other creatures. The Fungi from Yuggoth. The Mi-go."

"I'm familiar."

"Of course you are. The Appalachian Mountains stretch through both Point Pleasant and your hometown of Blairsville. An interesting connection, don't you think? But if I were to tell you that the Mothman is a hybrid, half Mi-go and half nightgaunt, you wouldn't believe me."

"Of course not."

"Is it because the Mi-go are supposed to be at war with the Elder Gods, and the nightgaunts serve the Elder Gods?"

"No, it's because there are no such things as Mi-go or nightgaunts. They're made-up creatures out of a book."

"However, if I told you there's a relationship between the Mothman and the Men in Black, you'd be more prone to believe me, even though they're characters in a comedy film starring Will Smith."

"That's different. Men in Black exist."

"Look, I know you think this whole Mothman legend is a load of manure. That's pretty obvious. I also know you've written a lot of articles on UFOs. I've read them. Honestly, how much do you *really* believe?"

"I wouldn't have said those things in my articles if I didn't believe them."

"Because you saw a UFO when you were a child."

"You did read my articles," Lawrence said.

"But don't you see how someone could also read those articles but go away thinking you didn't believe?"

"Not really."

"Look at it this way. You claim extraterrestrials have visited the Earth on a number of occasions. You also claim that forces, both terrestrial and extraterrestrial, don't want this to become common knowledge and have extraordinary methods at their disposal to make sure their secrets remain safe."

"That's right."

"If you really believe that, why did you write those articles? Aren't you worried that something will happen to you? That someone will try to silence you?"

"It's a possibility, but I can't worry about that. I have to get the truth out there. That's my job. It's my duty."

"Well said. Just so you know, I do believe you. That's why I'm here. What I have to say to you, it's much bigger than the truth about the Mothmen. And yes, there's more than one. I could tell you more about their connection to the Men in Black or fill you in on what was taken from the Ordinance Works the night the Silver Bridge fell. Something so important and so secret, the bridge was destroyed as a distraction to camouflage its removal. But that's nothing compared to the Truth. Do you understand what I'm offering here? I'm giving you the keys to the kingdom, lad. You've known all along there's been a coverup, the biggest conspiracy the world's ever known. But it goes deeper than even you could have possibly imagined. And I'm going to show you just how far it goes."

"How do I know you're telling the truth?" Lawrence asked.

"You're the investigative reporter. Maybe I'm full of malarkey. Never said I wasn't. It's your job to find out."

"Good point. Is this where I start my tape recorder?"

"If you'd like."

Lawrence pressed the record button on his digital recorder. The sensitive omnidirectional microphone plugged into it was already set up to record everything the two of them said.

"We were discussing the Truth," Lawrence said. "What exactly did you mean?"

"The Truth is based upon a single proposition, written in the form of a question: How is it that the world's worst-kept secrets also manage to be its best-kept ones?"

"Go on."

"It seems to make sense that the best way to keep any secret is to actually keep it secret. But do you understand how difficult that is? It's nearly impossible. And trying to silence anyone from revealing secrets is a logistical nightmare. The suspicion it would draw is one thing. The sheer number of people to go after is another thing entirely. Everyone knows about flying saucers, Area 51, even the Men in Black. In casual conversation, they might even say they believe some of it. But if you press them, really press them about it, most have to admit they don't believe much of it at all. That's true power."

"Mind control?"

"The greatest low maintenance mind control ever conceived."

"How does it work?"

"Its brilliance is in its simplicity. Magicians have known about this technique since time immemorial. They have an old saying: *if you want to hide something, paint it bright red*. The best way to protect any secret is to put it out into the open where no one can see it."

"But aren't they afraid someone will prove the stories to be true?"

"Of course not. They control how those stories are released to the public. But notice this. You didn't ask me who *they* are. You didn't need to. Everyone knows who *they* are. And yet they're perfectly safe. Why? Because if you tell people the Earth's gravity comes from its chewy caramel center, they'll laugh at you. But tell them loudly and long enough, and people will begin to doubt the Law of Gravity. Skepticism is a powerful tool of obfuscation. All you need to do is tell the truth with just enough bunkum to make people dismiss everything, truth and fiction. Cast David Duchovny to reveal your secrets every week on national television, and have him do it in front of a large poster that says *I Want To Believe*, just so you can laugh at the irony. And then, when someone starts to talk seriously about UFOs, someone else is sure to say, 'Oh, you mean like that television show.' The secret becomes a story, and no one takes it seriously."

"So the X-Files is part of an organized conspiracy to discredit ufology?"

"A part of it, yes, but there's so much more. It's been going on for centuries, all serving the same purpose."

"It's an interesting theory."

"See? I told you the truth, right to your face, and you don't believe me. I mention the X-Files and you won't listen to a word I say, even though you believe some of the things on that show are true. That's how strong the conditioning is."

"What you're saying, it's ridiculous."

"Isn't it, though?"

Lawrence shut off the recorder. "I appreciate your time."

"There's no point in getting angry, is there?"

"I don't know what you expect me to do."

"Then let me tell you. I expect you to do absolutely nothing. Don't you get it? You've always thought yourself outside the conspiracy, working to expose it. But you're just another gear in the machine, fitted into place the day you saw that UFO those many years ago. You won't expose anything. Quite the opposite. You *are* the conspiracy. You're a storyteller. A protector of secrets. Guardian of the Truth."

"That's not true."

"I think you know it is."

"If I can't change anything, then why tell me?"

"Since we're being honest, there was no reason to tell you anything. But how boring would that be? I have to admit, I do so enjoy the look on your face every time you realize the truth. I never get tired of seeing that look on your face."

"What?"

Mr. X stood and stretched. "I'd love to continue this fascinating conversation, but I have my work here to finish. Then I'll leave you to planning your interviews and attending the Mothman Festival. And when you go home, you'll write that new chapter for your book. And what fun you'll have writing it. It'll feel like the easiest piece you've ever written. It doesn't really matter what you write about. Write about how the Mothman was seen in Boca Raton, Florida, last year. Or about the witches coven in Pennsylvania that worships the Mothman as their Baphomet.

"Or, you could write about the strange gentleman you met in your hotel room, someone that didn't seem quite human. Suddenly, his eyes began to glow red and you realized that the words he spoke to you, which sounded like perfect English, were nothing more than a cacophony of inhuman clicks and whistles. But still you understood him. Only then did you realize he was a Man in Black, and when he unfurled his wings and revealed his true form, you realized he was so much more.

"You *could* write about that. Not that you would. Not that you're going to remember any of this. And your recorder doesn't have a thing on it. Again. You'll still write the truth, mostly, but no one will believe you. They'll label you a crackpot for the rest of your life. And that's good, because that's your job. It's your duty."

Lawrence called Mr. Keaton on Sunday before he left Point Pleasant.

"How did the interviews go?" Mr. Keaton asked.

"Fantastic. I tell you, I could write an entire book on the Mothman. I just might. The amount of new material I have is awe inspiring."

"That's great. I have to admit, I got the impression you weren't too enthusiastic about adding the Mothman chapter to your book."

"You kidding? It was a great idea. Don't know why I didn't think of it myself. Wait until you read the new chapter. I know you'll love it as much as I do."

"I'm sure I will. So, where did you find all this new information?"

"You know what they say," Lawrence said. "The truth is out there."

New Monster

By Lisa Morton

Maggie stared up at Mothman, and a happy shiver raced through her. She thought she knew every monster—she'd seen *House of Dracula* at least ten times, she owned every issue of *Famous Monsters* from #8 on, and she'd put together three monster models by herself—but she'd never heard of Mothman.

She studied the garish carnival banner and tried to imagine the eight-foot-tall creature with huge red bug eyes and iridescent wings fighting Frankenstein's monster or the Phantom. She wondered if there was a Mothman movie she'd never heard of, maybe something Spanish or Italian. The television at home only got four channels, and she knew there were a lot of movies she'd missed.

"Maggie!"

Turning, Maggie spotted her older sister, Sarah, searching for her through the midway crowd. Sarah, with her bell-bottoms and her boyfriend Todd; Sarah, who called Maggie a tomboy and made fun of horror movies. Sarah was supposed to be looking after Maggie today, even though Maggie had complained to their dad ("I'm thirteen, Dad. I can go to the carnival by myself!"); Maggie knew Sarah wasn't any happier with the arrangement than she was. She didn't exactly hate her sister, but Sarah was just so. . . *normal*. She liked The Beatles and hated books and wanted to marry Todd before 1970 and have her first baby by the time she was 20. Her hair was always perfect, she wore the latest fashions, and she had a lot of friends who were just like her.

She was everything Maggie would never be.

So Maggie turned her back and walked rapidly away until she saw a small group of people clustered around a tent opening, a barker standing before them on a platform. "See the Alligator-Skinned Man! Half-reptile, half-human, all weird and absolutely real, real, real! The Fat Lady, weighing in at nearly a thousand pounds of pure female! Gentlemen, that is a whole lot of woman! Feel the chill of fear as you gaze upon the Mothman, a weird winged beast captured somewhere in the hills of West Virginia—is it human or insect? You be the judge, ladies and gentlemen—all this for one quarter, only one thin quarter!"

Maggie dug in her pockets and pulled out her change—she had forty cents left, after buying an entrance ticket to the carnival, two rides (the Ferris wheel and the tilt-a-whirl), and a box of popcorn. She put the nickel and dime back in her pocket, thrust the quarter at a bored attendant, giving her admittance into the freak show.

The interior of the tent was dim, despite spotlights highlighting the various exhibits. Maggie, only mildly interested, walked past the Bearded Woman, the Mermaid (a long-dead looking thing in a filthy glass tank), and the Fat Lady, who was eating a candy bar. Maggie paused for a moment at the two-headed baby floating in a jar, but moved on.

At the rear of the tent was another banner for Mothman, next to a closed flap. Maggie started to push through, but a skinny man in a straw boater stepped forward and barred her entrance with a cane. "Ah-ah-ah, little lady, that'll be another ten cents if you want to see the Mothman."

Maggie knew better than to argue; besides, Sarah would never find her in there. She pulled her dime out, handed it to the man, and he pulled the cloth aside for her.

She stepped through into a small, even darker tent; she followed a glow off to her right, rounded a corner—and Mothman stood before her.

For a moment, Maggie's heart stopped. She stared up, up, her jaw pulling down. The thing before her was immense, with dark gray skin, a segmented torso, clawed fingers, bulbous red eyes and wide, tattered wings. It stood on a platform, arms outthrust, and Maggie instinctively took a step away from it. Could it have been real? In the half-light of the tent, it was hard to make out details. Forcing herself to look at it more carefully, she moved forward, started to reach out.

The eyes lit up.

Maggie jumped, startled, snatching her hand back. . . then she looked at the glowing crimson orbs and realized they were Christmas ornaments, big glass balls with red lights inside. Now she saw the wooden struts holding the figure up, the dust and cobwebs clinging to the aged fabric that made up the wings and the places where the gray leotard covering the mannequin had torn.

Fake.

It wasn't a real monster. Not even as real as John Carradine playing Dracula, or Boris Karloff as the Mummy. Mothman didn't even have a live actor inside; it was just a stuffed, oversized doll.

Maggie sagged in disappointment. She wanted to go back to the skinny man at the tent flap and ask for her dime back, but she knew he'd just laugh at her. Then she'd end up with Sarah and Todd, and they'd take her home and tease her about how much she liked movies and books, and tomorrow she'd be back at school, behind her desk in the last row as far away from the other kids as possible.

"Not very good, is it?"

Maggie whirled; she hadn't realized someone else had come into the tent. She saw a man behind her, strangely dressed in a dark business suit with white shirt and simple black tie; even weirder, though, were the sunglasses he wore in the shadowy tent. His brown hair was cut short and perfectly combed, almost *too* perfectly. Maggie knew she shouldn't talk to strangers, but his voice was pleasant and she agreed with the sentiment.

"It's pretty stupid."

The man didn't move; in fact, he stood so still that Maggie tried to see him breathing. His chest *was* moving in and out, wasn't it? And why was he here?

"Were you hoping it was real?" His head didn't even tilt as he spoke to her.

Maggie shrugged. "I guess."

"Wouldn't that have frightened you?"

"I like monsters."

Maggie began to wonder if something was wrong with him. What if he was sick, one of those crazies her sister called a perv? Maggie couldn't stifle a shiver, and she looked past him, startled to realize she couldn't see the place she'd come in through. "I better go—I think I just heard my sister."

She tried to move past him, and although he didn't physically stop her, his words did. "Would you like to see a real Mothman?"

She peered up at him and saw the barest hint of smile on his immobile face. "Well, yeah, but. . . they aren't real, so what's the difference?"

"The difference might mean a lot. . . to you."

Another chill arced up Maggie's spine. She wanted to leave—knew it was a mistake to stay here, that this wasn't safe—but she was trapped now by her own curiosity. "What do you mean?"

His head did turn just slightly towards her now, although his features remained implacable. "You're not like the other kids. You like monsters and carnivals and horror movies and Halloween, because you want to experience wonder. You look at the ones who are a little older than you, who already have boyfriends and marriage plans, and you think, Will that be me in a few more years? And you don't want it to be you...but you're secretly afraid that there might be no other way out of this town. So you escape by dreaming about Dracula and the Wolfman and ghosts."

Maggie was trembling slightly now; she'd never heard anyone talk about her like that. Everyone else just called her "weirdo" or "tomboy"; even her mom didn't know about the journals she kept under her bed, the ones she wrote monster stories in, complete with drawings it took her hours to make.

"Are you some kind of. . . mind-reader?"

His face twitched slightly. "No. I'm just someone who was. . . a lot like you once."

"But you're not now?"

"I got out."

What *was* he? Maggie ran through the possibilities in her head, and only one thing made sense: "Do you work for the government?"

"In a manner of speaking."

Maggie didn't know what that meant, but she was pleased that she'd guessed something almost right about him. "Did you come here to find out if Mothman was real?"

"You're a smart little girl. Yes, I did. I assumed it would be fake but had to be sure."

She swallowed, her throat suddenly dry, and asked, "Are there real ones somewhere?"

"What's your name?"

Did she dare risk giving him her name? Her mom had always told her not to talk to strangers, but she'd already told this man other things.

Surely it couldn't hurt just to tell him her first name, could it? If he was a perv, he couldn't track her down from that. "Maggie."

"Maggie, have you ever wondered why things like ghosts and UFOs and Mothman seem to appear and then vanish?"

"I never really thought about it, but. . . yeah, that's strange."

"Have you ever heard of alternate dimensions?"

She'd seen an episode of *Lost in Space* that had featured dimensional invaders; they'd looked like hairless disembodied heads with no mouths. "I think so."

"Imagine a world existing right next to ours, one full of monsters and ghosts and UFOs. There are windows between our world and that one, and sometimes these things can come through. We can't see the windows, but *they* can—so when they step back through into their own world, it looks like they've just disappeared."

Maggie's mind began to spin out new stories, possibilities, happenings…but one thing brought her thoughts to an abrupt, frustrated stop. "If we can't see the windows, then . . . we can't go through to their world."

"I'd like to show you something, Maggie." He stepped around into the darkness behind the Mothman display, and Maggie wondered if he had permission to go back there, then she realized he was waiting for her to follow.

This was when she should turn and run. Leave this tent, find safety. But safety meant a safe life, and Maggie didn't want a safe life, so she followed him.

The cloth side of the tent was right in front of them. He pushed out at it with one arm and made a sweeping motion, and Maggie couldn't be sure what he'd just done, if he'd pulled back only rough canvas or something more, because. . .

Beyond the tent was forest—dark, thick, primeval. Only a small clearing of a dozen feet separated them from the wall of shadows and trees. Maggie felt as if she was looking down rather than straight in front of her, down into some sort of thought given form, like the most basic fairy tale dredged up from somewhere unimaginably deep and brought to life.

There was something glowing among the branches, two circles of blood-hued glimmer. The circles floated forward, taking more shape. They were eyes. Around them appeared a man-sized insect face. Behind those eyes spread heavy wings with a pattern like a faded tapestry.

Mothman stood in the gloom of the trees. She could hear the flutter of his wings. He was immense—taller even than the cheap carnival mimicry and far stranger—with spindly, jointed arms and legs and a beetle-like torso. Maggie held her breath, somehow sure he would find her if she exhaled. He was real, not a movie monster but *real*, and she wasn't sure she wanted to be found.

He vanished. And Maggie was standing just inches from a worn canvas tent wall, gasping in air.

She also knew she was alone. The man in the suit had disappeared with Mothman.

She staggered away on wobbly knees, her breath coming quick and fast. When she bumped up against the display platform, she turned and looked up at the tawdry mannequin, and suddenly laughter erupted from her lungs. She saw the ridiculous lighted eyes and nearly doubled over in relief and joy and glee at what she'd been shown, the gift she'd been given.

After a while, when she'd stopped laughing and could walk again, she left the tent. The carny in the boater hat eyed her curiously as she stepped through the entrance flap again. "Like what you saw in there, kid?"

Maggie almost roared again, but she managed to tamp it down and merely grin. "Oh yeah. It was definitely worth ten cents."

The carny shook his head. "Are you high or what, kid?"

Maggie strode past him, heading out of the tent. Outside, Sarah would be waiting for her, and for the first time ever, that was okay. Because Maggie knew her life *would* be special. She even thought she might meet the man in the suit again someday, when she was older, and next time he'd take her through the window.

But for now, she had a new monster to add to her journals.

Lure of Water

By Victorya Chase

Jocelyn sat beneath a giant black oak and pushed her back against the trunk in an attempt to release the anger trapped in her spine. She'd remembered a bit about trees from biology class, something about how they transported waste through the branches to be expelled by the leaves. She wanted to transfer her pain to the tree to expel. Some things were hard for her to deal with on her own.

While she pushed, harder as her anguish increased, Jocelyn dug through her pockets. She had plenty of pockets. There were about six in her cargo pants and a few more on the military jacket she wore over her sweater. She stopped to stroke one finger on the name patch—Holt. She never knew him, picking up the jacket at an Army / Navy store, but pretended he loved her just the same. Jocelyn continued her search and pulled out a yellow box cutter. It was rusted; she had found it in a puddle at school about a week ago. Being a sophomore in high school was getting tougher, not the classes, but finding places to hide.

Jocelyn clicked the blade up until it was visible. She pulled her sweater across the blade to remove some of the rust, and then she moved the blade into her left hand and placed its tip on the lifeline in her right. She wasn't sure if she wanted to remove it or make it longer. What she did know was the tree wasn't working; she still hurt. Jocelyn pushed the point of the blade into her palm and watched a drop of blood travel down her lifeline. She pushed the blade deeper and pulled it along her palm. Then she removed the blade, clicked it closed, and watched the blood seep from lifeline to loveline. Nearby was a creek; she could hear it call to her through her pain. She walked toward it, grass crisping beneath her steps, the smell of encroaching winter filling her senses.

Like a moth to the flame, such was Jocelyn's inability to escape the lure of water. She had to step in every puddle, every river or stream and look down into its ripples. Now she squatted beside the creek, put her hands in its icy cold, and watched her blood swirl. She looked down and saw the face of her sister. As much as Jocelyn was lured by the water, Jessica was even more so. Every rain Jess would strip down and dance, not coming in until their father cocooned her in a thick blanket and dragged her kicking and screaming inside.

Jocelyn fought to find herself in the reflection. She lifted her hand; the wound had stopped bleeding but was an angry red. She closed her eyes and willed tears to flow. She never cried after Jess decided life was too much without the water, that the waves of the Ohio River were more welcoming than those of Jocelyn who held her every night, rocking her and whispering that she understood but needed her more than the river gods.

What is the worth of one twin? The power is in the pair. With Jess gone, who was Jocelyn? Jocelyn's father cried after Jess was dragged from the river, hair a tangled mess, face pale white, dead emerald eyes staring up at the sky and her smile beatific as the rain fell and caressed their angel. He held on to Jocelyn and sobbed giant tears that rolled from his face into her hair, damp from her father's grief and the opening heavens. He choked out how he couldn't understand it, first his wife and now his daughter. He sobbed that he saw the curse in her, yet he also saw strength to break away from it. Every woman in her family had drowned with a smile.

Jocelyn took out the box cutter and used it to prick her fingers. She knew what the water's embrace would do to her and tried to understand why her father stopped holding her after Jess died. There was no one left for her now. Jocelyn wrapped her jacket tighter around herself and looked out across the creek. There she saw an abnormality, an oak with a wide protrusion on its trunk. She pressed her bloody fingertips against Holt's name and dreamt it was his arms around her, not her own thin ones.

The object was a chrysalis, or cocoon. The name depended on what was housed within. Jocelyn preferred the term chrysalis, never liking that a moth wasn't beautiful enough to be housed inside something with a nice name. Like the way she was called Joe despite the beauty of her real name. Her teachers had shortened her name long ago, as had her family. While she didn't mind when her mother in her soft alto or sister in crystal clear soprano sang out her name when she was wanted, she hated the flatness of 'Joe' on anyone else's lips.

Jocelyn walked around the chrysalis. It was as big as a man, if not six foot from tip to tip close to that. The brown matched the oak, although the striations differed. She imagined what it must be like to be able to coat yourself with your own silken saliva and hide from life. It was a form of time travel she wished she possessed. She lay her ear against the rough surface and listened for movement but found none. A chrysalis that big could take forever to hatch. Jocelyn sat down and leaned her back against the hardened silk, pushing herself against it. She felt some give and prayed that the chrysalis would accept the loneliness that was killing her.

Jocelyn woke when the chrysalis began to move. It was a gentle pushing from the inside. She wondered how moths and butterflies normally got out. She'd seen chickens hatch before and knew they used their beaks, but what would a giant moth have? She stood up and felt around the chrysalis.

"Hello," she said, "are you okay in there?"

The movement stopped and Jocelyn heard muffled coos. She kept one hand on the chrysalis and felt whatever was inside push up against it. With her other hand she found the box cutter. She took it in her right hand, still an open wound, and clicked the blade up.

"I can help you," she said, "I think." Her blood had dried on the blade, a darker red than the burnt umber rust.

"Just stand back a bit, if you can," she said, pushing the blade against the outside of the shell. Again whatever was inside met her hand. It began to coo louder, a deep innocent sound. She walked around to where chrysalis met tree and placed her left hand as far away from that seam as possible. Whatever was inside was pushing harder now. With her right hand she carefully placed the thin blade between the tree and the chrysalis, prying it free. The being inside continued to push against her hand, and she cooed back that everything would be okay. Once she had cut a big enough opening she put her hand in and began pulling the object from the tree, the sound like tearing paper, like waves singing her name.

The creature pushed against the seam until both collapsed on a fresh dusting of snow. Jocelyn realized this was the wrong time for any insect to hatch, and that was her first thought before realizing what lay next to her gagging, coughing, and trying to move.

A Mothman.

His wings were crumpled against his body, which was mostly human, though covered with silky gray hairs. He shivered. Jocelyn brought him to a clearing by the creek to let the winter sun warm him. She wondered if he was thirsty.

"What are you?" she asked, even though she knew the stories. The

Mothman came when tragedy was near. He had been around when the Silver Bridge collapsed. But where was he when her sister died? Her mother? Her grandmother? Why was he so late? She examined him closely, running her hands up his chest to his face—covered with the same soft fur. He had two antennae atop his head and red streaks around them told her that her lifeline had reopened. He turned his head to look at Jocelyn. Crimson eyes burned out of his face so close to human, the eyes just too far apart to be normal, a nose so short as to be just holes in his face, and a cotton candy pink mouth that was still gasping, fighting for words.

The Mothman pushed his hands against the ground and fell into them. Jocelyn took one hand in hers and held it there, rubbing warmth into the newly hatched fingers. Still he shivered, shaking terribly in the pre-winter cold. Jocelyn realized that he needed to open his wings— that was how he could get stronger. If he just opened them and let the sun stream through, he would gain the strength to do what he needed.

"My name is Jocelyn. Joe," she said in as soft a voice as she could, not wishing to startle him. The Mothman gasped again.

"You're probably thirsty," she continued, "being so long in there without water." She moved closer to the creek and looked in, once more seeing her sister look back. Jocelyn closed her eyes and reached in with one cupped hand, through the reflection, and brought some water to the Mothman's lips. It drank greedily, soft flesh and fur brushing against her palms. She kept bringing up handfuls of water until his gasping died down. He breathed heavily and stretched out his wings, translucent enough for thin veins to show, roadmaps to the secrets he alone knew. One completely covered Jocelyn who lay next to him. She felt the fragility and warmth even through her jacket, fingered Holt's name, and fell asleep.

The moon shone bright, turning the ripples of the creek into splashing black diamonds. The Mothman was standing. Jocelyn shook off her dreams of Jess, of diving into the waves to once more be held by her mother and sister. They had always been together; it was Jess and Joe until suddenly it was just Joe and a father who cried giant tears and a river that whispered sweet nothings to her. She pushed herself into a seated position and stared up at the Mothman, watching him test out his wings. She watched him move his mouth as if to speak, but only a squeaking purr escaped.

"I'll call you Holt," Jocelyn said. Holt took a few steps, stumbling. His mouth moved again, like he was trying to say the name.

"Holt," Jocelyn said. The Mothman's mouth moved once more, then he sat down beside her.

"You're too late anyway," she said, taking his hand and placing it in hers.

"You're too late," she said again. She fought to cry, but the tears refused to come. "You're too late," she said once more, her voice barely a whisper. The Mothman ran his finger over her torn lifeline. Jocelyn watched his expression change from confusion to sadness. She pushed his hand away and stood.

"Why are you here?" she suddenly screamed. "Why now? My mother is already gone, my sister gone. Everyone I loved is gone! Why now? Why not before—to warn us? I would have listened! I would have listened and not let Jessica wander off. I wouldn't have let her out of my sight!"

The Mothman reeled back and placed his hands over his antenna. Jocelyn walked closer to him.

"I'm sorry, Holt," she said, reaching out a hand. "I'm sorry I yelled.

I just don't understand."

The Mothman took her hand, and she sunk into him, burying her head in his chest. He wrapped his arms and wings around her, lowering his head into her hair.

The fog was so thick, when Jocelyn looked through the kitchen window, she couldn't see if the car was in the driveway. She was used to the comfort of her father's forest green jeep in front of the house. Even if he couldn't look at her without crying, his presence at least let her know she wasn't alone in her grief. Jocelyn walked outside and saw his jeep wasn't there. She rubbed the name patch on her jacket and wondered how Holt was doing. She didn't want to take him home that night, anger and confusion too strong. Jocelyn was determined to visit him today and hoped he stayed by the creek like she told him. After school she planned to go and apologize, to ask him why he was here and offer to help. She would be the voice he didn't have.

The fog didn't lift even as the sun struggled to break through the clouds. Usually a morning fog didn't last this long. The water in the air embraced Jocelyn while she walked to school. It whispered to her secrets of a damp heaven. A fire drill gave her the peace she needed from endless classes, teachers droning until there voices were no more than the wind across an ocean, dull whispers that settled in the back of her mind while she doodled and waited for the day to end.

Jocelyn stepped in puddles around the trashcans, watching the ripples distort reflections—her shoe, her pants, and the gray sky.

"My mother died when I was young," a voice said. Jocelyn turned to see Amy, a friend closer to Jess than herself. "I miss her," Amy continued. "I miss Jess, too."

Jocelyn turned away and searched her pockets for the box cutter.

She clicked the blade up and down.

"It can't be easy," Amy said. "Really, I know it can't be easy. With my mother, well, it's still hard."

"How insightful," Jocelyn replied, anger rising.

"I guess it's even harder for you. But, well, I'm still your friend."

Jocelyn resented Amy. Resented that she was coming to her now, months after Jess's passing. Everything was happening too late. Where was Amy right after? Where was she when Jocelyn's sister left, not even a year after their mother? Where was the understanding then?

"Leave me alone," Jocelyn said. She walked out of the schoolyard, past the other students, past teachers too busy talking to each other to notice that she was already at the chain-link fence looking back, silently pleading to be seen, praying for the release her sister found as fervently as she prayed to not follow in her footsteps.

When she found herself standing at the shore of the Ohio River, Jocelyn realized everything was futile. She removed the box cutter from her pocket and slashed it across her lifeline. With each cut she heard her sister's laughter, saw her mother's smile. When the hot blood seeped up she felt their arms around her and was once again at the lake, swimming past the point of exhaustion, holding their hands while they all danced through puddles and splashed through the rain. But it was never enough. No one loved the women in her family like the water did. No matter how hard her father tried, it wasn't enough. She took another step forward and felt the waves lap against her ankles. She took another step, and then another. Jocelyn dropped the box cutter and a wave stole it away.

"Holt," Jocelyn said, rubbing her bloody fingers across the name patch. She closed her eyes, hung her head, and walked into the waves.

A rustling sound stopped her. She turned around to see red eyes glowing through the fog, a lighthouse of moth and man at the shore.

"Holt?" A flutter was her answer. The ruby gaze grew stronger while he moved through the fog. The river fought back, stronger now, as the water reached out and begged her to join her sister.

"Holt? Why?" she asked, her foot stepping backward, the wave's whispers strengthening even as the intense ruby eyes begged that she stop.

A hand reached through the fog, strong and slick, covered as it was in silk and dew. Jocelyn grabbed it and felt the warmth he offered. The waves lapped harder now, pulling at her feet, the mud sucking at her shoes.

Jocelyn began to cry. Tears poured down her face. She collapsed and the Mothman caught her and lifted her in his arms. She leaned her head to his chest and listened to his heartbeat. Salt water trickled down his body as tears for her sister finally escaped. She gasped for air, the force of the released pain and grief making it hard to breathe. Holt flew away from the river, away from the grave of Jocelyn's ancestors, and to her home. There he stood holding her—the fog a thick cocoon around them both—until headlights pierced through, and Jocelyn heard the familiar rumbling of her father's jeep. The vehicle screeched to a stop, and he ran out of the car.

"Joe!" he yelled.

Jocelyn's father ran up and stopped just in front of the Mothman. Jocelyn watched him search for an explanation. The Mothman set Jocelyn down and her father grabbed her away and into an embrace so full of love and loss that she started crying again. Her father's tears joined hers.

"Oh Joe, the school called me, the fire drill—" her father choked out. "Joe, when they called. . . I can't lose you, Joe. Oh my sweet Jocelyn, I'm so sorry."

Jocelyn turned around to look once more at the Mothman still standing in their driveway.

"Thank you, Holt," she whispered.

Jocelyn reentered her father's embrace. The sound of wings moving told her Holt was gone forever now, but her father's tears told her he had come just in time.

A Night for Mothing

By Orrin Grey

Casey parked the truck a ways back from the house and killed the lights. For a while he just sat, watching the house through the night. There weren't any streetlights this far out, but the peeling paint of the old house itself seemed to glow in the dark like some luminous fungus. When he'd watched long enough, he got the shotgun down from the rack behind the seat, made sure it was loaded, and then started across the wet grass.

The house was big, sprawling, quasi-Victorian, like a lot of the old houses this far out of town. It had belonged to Reggie's grandma before she died, and Casey's mom said it had been nice once, back when the old lady still lived there. Before Reggie moved in and ruined it, the same way he ruined everything he touched, the same way he'd ruined Jennifer.

Casey thought of her the way she'd been when he saw her last: lying in the hospital bed, one eye swollen shut, her lips split and crusted with blood, her skin pale and slick, waiting until their mom was out of the room to beg him, "Please, Casey, please go get the stuff from Reggie's. I need it."

Whatever she needed, Casey knew that wasn't it, and he didn't have any intention of getting it for her. So why had he come? He didn't know. Maybe just an excuse to get away, to keep from walking down the cold white hospital hall and finishing the job he'd started. When Reggie came to their mom's house looking for Jennifer, he'd found Casey instead. On the front lawn, Casey'd delivered a beating that landed Reggie in intensive care and would have landed Casey in jail for the night, or longer, except for Sheriff Logan. The sheriff knew

Casey's mom, had seen Casey and Jennifer grow up, had seen Jennifer loaded into the ambulance, and knew what had driven Casey's fists.

It wasn't the beating that Reggie'd given her that had put Jennifer in the hospital. She was withdrawing from whatever drug they'd been on together, the drug that Reggie'd supplied her until she tried to leave him, the "stuff" she was begging Casey to bring her. The same stuff that'd made her thin and clammy, that turned her eyes as red as Christopher Lee's in one of those old Dracula movies that they used to watch together on Saturday nights when they were kids, telling her when the scary parts were over so she could uncover her eyes.

Casey had known that Reggie was trouble from the start, but what could he do? Jennifer was a grown woman now, going to community college, and Reggie was something of a legend there, the guy who could get you what you needed. Casey had gone around when Jennifer first moved in with him, intending to put the fear of God into him, but Reggie wasn't the type to get scared easy, not without getting hurt bad first, and Jennifer had begged Casey, pushed him, told him that if he laid a hand on Reggie she'd never speak to him again.

That'd been enough to stop him then. Now it was too late.

Casey stepped up onto the front porch, feeling the step give under his weight. The porch light was on, and moths were beating themselves against it, their furry bodies making tiny *thup, thup* sounds against the plastic dome. He tried the door and found it locked, but the windows were open to the summer heat, and Casey had no trouble slipping in through one of them.

The furniture in the living room was mostly what had been left by Reggie's grandma. Old-fashioned stuff with wooden legs and faded floral patterns, stained with old smoke, spilled booze, and God knew what else. Trash and old laundry littered the floor, and the pictures had been pulled down off the walls, replaced by things torn out of magazines, or by nothing at all. There were candles burnt down to puddles of wax on almost every surface, and the smell of the place, even with the windows thrown wide, was a bouquet of incense, sweat, and pot, undercut by subtler smells of rot and other things that Casey couldn't identify.

He walked across the living room, leading with the shotgun, his finger not quite on the trigger, but ready to be. The TV was on, strobing the room in cold silvery radiance, but the sound was muted. Again, Casey wondered what he was doing. Trespassing, stretching the leniency that the law had already shown him. If he'd wanted to go to jail, he should have just gone down to Reggie's hospital room and held a pillow over his face until he stopped thrashing.

But then he thought of Jennifer, the image of her in the hospital bed. He thought about the promise he'd made to their mom that he'd look out for her. He thought about the nurses in the hospital, shaking their heads and whispering about "these kids today," because they couldn't figure out what the drug in her system was whose presence or lack was maybe killing her.

Maybe if he could figure out what the "stuff" that Jennifer wanted was, maybe then he could still help her, still watch out for her as he'd failed to do before now. That's what he told himself as he walked through the house, going room to room, finding a lot of bad stuff, but nothing unexpected or new.

The house was deserted, and all the interior doors were open, except one in the kitchen that he figured led down into the basement. It had a shiny new padlock.

He got a knife out of one of the drawers and rested the shotgun against the cabinet while he pried the latch out of the old wood. He froze with his hand on the gun when it jumped loose with a loud pop, but if anyone or anything heard, they made no sign. He dropped the knife into the overflowing trashcan, so it wouldn't be lying out handy, and then he went downstairs, the shotgun once more leading the way.

As soon as he opened the door, he knew he'd found something bad, something new. There was a smell in the basement that was different than the rest of the house, like nothing he'd ever smelled before. It made him think of things like dried flowers and the first girl he'd ever kissed, but he couldn't have said what it smelled *like* to save his life.

The stairs going down into the basement were wooden, the kind with openings for something to stick its hand through and trip you as you were going down, but a switch on the stairwell filled the basement with light, warm and yellow. Oil lamps hung from the ceiling, and old tools hung on the unfinished walls, all stuff that had been left there since Reggie's grandma died, no doubt.

The basement floor was concrete with a drain in the center and a sump pump in one corner. The rest of the room was dominated by a long wooden table with a bench on one side and chairs on the other. And in the darkest corner, an iron cage sized for a Rottweiler held something that wasn't a dog.

At first he thought it was a kid, that they had a kid in a cage, but no, it wasn't as bad as that, and at the same time it was worse. They had a *thing* in a cage. A shadow, shaped like a child except for the ragged wings, the low mound of a head, the eyes. He knew what it was, of course, as soon as he saw it, *really* saw it. He'd heard stories. Who hadn't? Lover's lane tales of the Mothman. His friend Wayne swore to have seen it once, just a black shape, like a bat, and those burning eyes.

Casey recognized it, though it was smaller than he'd heard and little more than a faded copy of the thing from the stories. Its wings hacked up and its eyes reduced to lusterless stones. Its arms and back stippled with black, bare places where it had brushed up against the bars of the cage, where the iron had burned off the fine silvery hairs that covered its body.

On the long table were all the tools they'd used to harvest from it. Razors, plastic bags, a scaling knife. And, sitting in the basket of a scale, a pile of gray powder, like makeup, shot through with glittering flecks like bits of quartz. The "stuff," Casey knew, and he gagged, choked, almost threw up in front of the thing in the cage.

He could see it now. The thing, wounded—hit by a car, maybe, or clipped by a hunter's rifle. Found, caught in the headlights of Reggie's car on the side of the road some moonless night. Caught, loaded up, and then hauled here, trapped here, held in the iron cage that burned with its touch, to have its wings cut down, ground up to make the powder they sniffed, snorted, shot, whatever. And, standing there, Casey could even imagine what the high must be like. Just from the smell, from the memories it stirred in him, he could imagine what it must be like to pull that inside, what it must feel like to transform, to become something more than what you were. He could imagine what the addiction must be like, the need to get that feeling back.

Jennifer had stood here, he knew. Stood and seen what he was seeing. Been a party to this terrible thing. Had she helped to trap it, helped to load it into the cage? Had her hands held the knife that scraped the scales from its wings? If they hadn't, then they may as well have.

The Mothman shuffled, but didn't make a sound, didn't speak or gasp or warble, just stared at him with those dull, unblinking eyes. He raised the shotgun, stepped toward the cage, but the creature didn't flinch, didn't move away. It looked at him, and he knew that if he pulled the trigger then it would welcome the death he brought.

He stood like that for a long time before lowering the gun. He cast around for a key to the cage, and when he didn't find it, he unloaded the shotgun, dropping the shells into his pocket, and used the stock of it to break the lock. He flinched with every clang of metal, but no one ever came.

When the lock was off, he opened the cage and stepped back. The Mothman stood and stared at him. Up close, here in the light, with it so reduced, it wasn't much to look at. More moth than man, its mouth a working mass of moving parts, its hands feathery and four-fingered. Slowly, slowly it crept forward, slipping out of the cage, the ragged stumps of its wings dragging against the metal. He saw the pain cross its inhuman features, but still it crept out, and as he stepped farther back it moved toward the stairs, slowly, deliberately, like a very old man.

Casey gathered up all the powder that was on the long table into one of the plastic bags, carried it upstairs, and flushed it down the first toilet he found. Then he slipped back out through the window he'd come in and walked around to the back lawn. The Mothman had made its way outside, but it couldn't fly with the ruins that remained of its wings. It just skulked away, into the pines behind the house.

Maybe it would heal out there. Casey didn't know what it was, didn't know what a thing like it was capable of recovering from. Maybe it would just crawl away and die in the hollow of a tree or in a grassy ditch. But not in a cage, anyway. He could give it that much, at least, and as he stood, watching Reggie's only real victim creep away, he was as close to peace as he'd been in a long time.

A Change in Direction

By Jessie Grayson

Gerri Andrews almost slammed on the breaks, but she decided to push the gas instead and run the punk over.

Over the last few weeks a sort of mass hysteria had broken out in town with the sightings. People were afraid to drive at night, to be alone anywhere remote, even the number of regulars at the bar Gerri tended had dwindled, biting into her meager tips and straining her budget, making her wonder what to do.

So she drove through the thick forest toward her apartment at three in the morning as usual, on a rainy night that was normal for this time of year, expecting to see nothing. But there it was.

In the headlights she caught a glimpse of the tall, dark figure standing in the middle of the road. Red glinted at the eyes. Wings seemed to flap out from the sides.

Gerri almost stopped.

She felt her chest tighten, just a little. Her stomach grew a bit unsteady as the hundreds of overheard conversations flooded back. How seeing *him* was a sign of terrible things to come. How those who did were doomed to suffering. But she'd been there, done that and it had nothing to do with this.

She gunned her car forward.

The figure stood, the distance shrinking while Gerri held her course. The idiot, probably a bored teenager like she had been a couple of years ago, would jump out of the way.

But he didn't move.

And she didn't waver as the space grew shorter.

Shorter.

She could see it clear in the headlight. Dark cloth, red eyes. Wings. My God, they looked like real wings. And the eyes, not glasses with red tint. Fur. Black fur.

She jerked the wheel to swerve but too late. She felt her car jolt and saw the body fly over her windshield. She slammed the breaks, skidding to a halt and turned in the seat. In the red glow of taillights she could see the thing lying very still.

Putting a hand to her chest, she felt her heart hammering against her palm. Without thinking she swung the door open and ran to the limp pile on the asphalt. She paused a foot from it, watching it heave breath. Glancing around, she found a limb off a tree beside the road and grabbed it.

Easing forward, limb first, she poked what appeared to be its side, and when it made no move she edged forward. Using her foot she nudged it over and stepped back. There it was. A Mothman—maybe she couldn't really tell, it could have been a Mothwoman. But it was real.

Gerri sat in the car, gripped the steering wheel so hard her knuckles turned white. Only minutes had passed but everything had changed, even the weather. The rain stopped and the sky began clearing, allowing weak moonlight to filter through thick clouds.

She chewed her bottom lip, debating. She had turned the car around, shining the headlight that wasn't busted on the Mothman, and she sat staring at it. She could smell the sweat mixed with stale smoke and bad booze from 'tending all night. She hated that job, the pay wasn't worth the drive anymore, but there wasn't anything else here. She could sell the thing for money. But who was on the market for Mothmen? Besides, what would she do with the money? Where would she go?

She put her forehead on the steering wheel. She could run it over, kill it and end this nonsense. It could be hurt. She glanced up at the damp heap, still breathing but not moving. But it hadn't done anything to her to deserve that and the thought made a sour taste settle on her tongue.

Still, she wasn't going to load it into her car and take it for healing. She'd seen that movie and it didn't end well for the driver.

Leave it. Her logical mind said. *Drive to the apartment and forget this ever happened.*

But it had happened.

She opened the door, stepped out into the cold rain and walked to the Mothman.

At its side, Gerri wiped her palms dry and took a firm grip on the stick. She hefted it like a ball bat and put a foot to the thing's back. "Hey? What now? Are you listening? Wake up and tell me something, do something. What am I supposed to do with you? What do I do now?"

She lowered the limb, gritting her teeth and feeling her chest burning with breathing too fast. She wiped her cheek, surprised to find it damp. Hadn't it stopped raining?

No movement came from the Mothman; it was as lifeless as the town she'd ended up in—breathing but just barely, and probably about to die. And it would take her down with it; she could feel herself wearing thin just to keep up with bills and work. When she'd left home, this wasn't what she'd expected.

She'd had a plan, but the guy she centered that plan on walked out two months in, and she couldn't just crawl back to her mother and the "I told you so" that was waiting.

Maybe there was nothing to do but give in. Let the town suck the life from her, let the Mothman have its way.

She felt the stick fall from her hand, and it clattered on the pavement.

The figure jerked upright.

She jumped backwards as the creature screamed, spread both wings, and rose to its feet. The thing loomed over her, shuddering, screaming again, and then began cracking. It shuffled one step toward her and broke into small pieces.

Gerri held her breath as the pieces tinkled to the road, forming a pile like busted glass. But this glass moved. Fluttered. Then, thousands of black moths lifted into the air.

Gerri watched the dark butterflies until they vanished into the cloudy night sky, leaving nothing behind. She leaned on her car hood. The wet metal felt cool against her back, and her head spun a little but felt clearer all at once.

Crawling inside the car, she gazed at the direction she was facing. Back into town, toward the interstate, which led across the state line and to her mom. It had been over a year and that felt like too long.

She put the car in gear, wondering when she'd busted her headlight out, and drove. *Probably some jerk at the bar*, she thought. She could maybe get her old job back at the diner and save up for college like Mom had wanted. She could get everything worked out. She knew what to do now.

The Young Lochinvar

By William Meikle

Julia really wanted to see a *real* Scotchman.

Edinburgh had been a *big* disappointment. Sir Walter Scott had led her to believe there would be cultured men in fine lace and kilts, young Lochinvars ready to sweep her off her feet and dance her away to a romantic retreat where she would be smothered in soft kisses. Instead, all she got were grey streets, fog and the taste of stale beer on a drunkard's lips.

Maybe Dundee will be better.

The signs were not proving good so far. The train clattered through a blustery dark night where the wind caused the carriages to sway alarmingly like a boat tossed by the waves. The sound assaulted her ears, and she yearned for the peace and quiet of their Chelsea drawing room. Pater only made things worse with his constant prattling about guns and shooting. When the other men in the carriage lit up their briar pipes in unison, Julia excused herself and left for the relatively clearer air in the corridor.

She hoped for a view from a window, something to raise her spirits, a glimpse of some *real* Scotchmen, or even some of the scenery on the subject of which Scott had waxed so eloquently. But night had fallen since the train departed Edinburgh and any excitement Julia might have got at crossing the Forth was lost in the rain and dark. Nothing could be seen beyond the window but gray, interspersed with rivulets of water where rain splashed and was smeared by the wind.

Welcome to Scotland.

She had only thought it, but a dark figure standing where the carriages met turned towards her. He stood with a light behind him, and his features lay in dark shadow. All she could tell was that he was tall and dressed in what looked like an expensive woolen overcoat.

"Your first time here, Miss?"

His voice was soft, almost timid, but Julia felt heat rising at her cheeks.

He's a Scotchman.

Yet again, although she had not spoken, he seemed to guess her intent.

"That would be *Scotsman,*" he said. "But no, I am only a visitor here."

"As am I," Julia replied, amazed at her own boldness. She looked back to the carriage. Pater was watching her closely, but he would not be able to see this stranger from where he sat. *If I keep my back to the carriage, Pater will never even know I am speaking.*

"And how do you like this country?" the tall man said. His voice sounded somewhat muffled, as if coming from a much further distance.

"I like what I have seen of it just fine," she replied. "But I wish this dashed rain would ease."

"I like the rain," the man said. "And the wind. It reminds me that I am but a servant of the elemental, not a master." What he said next was obscured as the train blasted through a short tunnel, but it had sounded like a series of numbers, ending in five and seventy.

"I'm sorry," she said. "I did not catch that."

He didn't reply, merely stood stock still. Although she could not see his eyes she felt his gaze on her like a physical force, and once again she blushed.

Her embarrassment quickly turned to confusion as the man spoke again.

"Five and seventy, three score and fifteen, a long span come to a sudden end, as they all do, in darkness and turmoil. It's coming yet, for a' that."

She might have been so bold as to question the man about his meaning, but at that moment a conductor arrived in the corridor to check tickets, and when she turned back there was no sign of the tall stranger. She considered walking through to the next carriage to see where he had gone, but she knew that if she left Pater's line of sight, for even a second, it would be noted and a reprimand would not be long behind.

She reluctantly returned to her Pater's party. For almost an hour, she kept a close eye on the corridor, but the tall man did not reappear. By the time the train stopped at Kirkcaldy, she had almost given up hope.

Her dismay was doubled when three young men in tweeds and plus fours boarded and Pater invited them in to the carriage.

"Julia," he said, as a youth with an overbite and a terrible case of acne sat opposite her. "I would like you to meet George Kerr. His father works with me in the City. He is to be your husband."

At first she thought she had misheard, but the look in Pater's eye told her he was deadly serious. She knew better than to make a scene in company, and forced herself to sit through George's, frankly embarrassing, attempts to prove his worth.

"I am so glad to finally meet you," the youth said. His voice, when compared to the gentle softness of the man in the corridor, felt like razors in her ears. "Your father has told me all about you."

Oh, I do hope not.

"Have you been on this line before?" he asked and continued without waiting for a reply. "It's a marvel of modern engineering. Our fathers helped build it, you know?"

And without waiting again, he kept on flapping his lips. Julia tuned him out as he spent ten minutes telling her how much iron, stone, and manpower went into the building of the new bridge at Dundee, the biggest, longest and most expensive ever built, and how an American president, no less, had called it "a big bridge for a small city." That remark caused much hilarity among George and his companions, leading them to bray like excited horses.

I cannot marry such as this. But what am I to do? I must follow my Pater's guide in these matters.

"We shall be at the bridge in thirty minutes or so," George said. "Isn't it exciting?"

Julie couldn't think of a suitable reply that would not seem disinterested, so she kept quiet. But she could not sit there any longer. When the train pulled in to Cupar station she excused herself, citing the need for air, and went to stand out in the corridor. A blast of cold wind came from an open exterior door, bringing with it the smell of rain. Now that the train was standing still at the platform, the full force of the gale outside could be both heard and felt. The whole carriage rocked and reeled.

"Welcome to Scotland, Miss," the soft voice said from her left. Once again he stood with the light at his back such that his face was hidden in shadow. "How are you enjoying it so far?"

She felt like running to him. . . throwing herself into his arms, giving no thought to the consequences. But she could almost feel Pater's gaze at her back, holding her rigid in her place, defining the flow of her life for the long stretch of future to come.

"It is not what I imagined," she said softly.

"*Love swells like the Solway, but ebbs like its tide,*" the tall man whispered in return.

"Do not tease me with Scott," she said, suddenly angry. "Not when Pater has betrothed me to. . . to. . ."

"*I come in peace to dance at your bridal,*" he said, his voice like soft silk.

Julia was in no mood for games.

"What is it that you want of me, sir?" she said, raising her voice to be heard above the wind that suddenly rose up a notch.

"What is it that you want of me?" the soft voice replied.

Her heart knew the answer, and beat ever faster. But Pater was still watching, and she could not bring herself to disobey him quite so openly.

Not yet.

A small voice had said that in her mind, but it seemed her tall companion had once more guessed her intentions.

"I will be here," he said. "I will always be here. Five and seventy, three score and fifteen, a long span come to a sudden end, as they all do, in darkness and turmoil. It's coming yet, for a' that."

She wanted to go to him, but Pater's gaze continued to hold her.

The tall man acted for her. He moved forward, so close that she might touch him if she chose. She still could not see his face, but she felt his soft breath at her cheek as he leaned towards her and planted a kiss there, cold and dusty, but a kiss nonetheless.

She heard movement behind her and turned. Pater was already out of his seat and coming towards her. He pulled the carriage door open with such force that it slammed hard against the wall, the noise echoing in the corridor even above the wind.

"You must go," she said, and then realized her companion had already left. She looked up and down the corridor, but there was no sign of him.

"Was that a man?" Pater said, the anger red in his face. "Was it?"

Pater dragged her back inside the carriage. As he pulled the door closed behind him, the train pulled out of Cupar Station.

Over the next ten minutes, Julia tried very hard to keep her attention on George, but the youth just could not stop talking about his prowess at shooting, his ability to make money, his horses, his dogs, even his taste in leather footwear. She was already weary of him.

And Pater wants me to spend years like this?

George finally realized that he did not have Julia's full attention, and the look of anger that crossed his face told her more than she needed to know about him. She resolved that she would have it out with Pater as soon as they were alone. She could *never* marry this boy.

Not when there is a man in the corridor waiting for me.

The thought came unbidden, but she found it to be most agreeable and lost herself in a reverie of thoughts of soft voices and even softer kisses. She was brought back to harsh reality when Pater poked her in the ribs.

"What is the matter with you tonight, girl? Young George here has asked you a question. Please at least have the good manners to answer him."

She blushed.

"I am sorry, Pater," she said, the lie coming easily to her lips. "I was just excited at the thought of the bridge."

Across the carriage from her, George's scowl turned quickly to a broad smile. He stood and reached for her hand. "Then come. We are almost there. We shall watch from the window."

His hand felt like a cold sausage as he took her by the wrist and led her out to the corridor. Her tall companion was nowhere to be seen and she felt her heart sink.

George in the meantime had become as excited as a puppy at walk-time.

But far less endearing.

"It is a great wonder. The cylindrical cast iron columns supporting the long span of the bridge are each seventy-five yards long, and Thomas Bouch received a knighthood for the design," he said. "Imagine. A knighthood."

She could indeed imagine. She was thinking of her tall stranger again.

There never was a knight like the young Lochinvar.

George failed to notice her lack of interest and led her to a window on the far side away from the wind and rain. Here, the sound of the wheels on the rails was more audible, even above the storm.

George was still lost in his own monologue.

"We should see the lights of the city across the river from here. 'Tis a pity it is so inclement. It is a fine view by moonlight."

There was a movement in the corridor behind them, little more than a slight dimming of the light, but Julia turned eagerly, anticipating her *Lochinvar.*

George tugged at her wrist, dragging her closer towards the window. "What is the matter with you, girl?"

The tone, the assumption of *ownership* so exactly mirrored that of her Pater that Julia pulled herself away, almost dragging them both off balance as the train *lurched*.

The wheels screeched on the rails and metal squealed.

The tall stranger was suddenly by her side, as if from nowhere. And now she could see his eyes, pale blue and infinitely sad in a dark-skinned face that spoke of long days under the sun.

"Will you come, lass? It is time. Five and seventy, three score and fifteen, a long span come to a sudden end, as they all do, in darkness and turmoil. It's coming yet, for a' that."

The carriage suddenly fell sideward, throwing George and Julia off balance. She found herself in the arms of the stranger, suddenly warm and cozy.

"What is it that you want of me?" he whispered.

She glanced at George. He was too busy clinging desperately to a wildly swaying door to pay her any attention.

"The poor craven bridegroom said never a word," the tall stranger intoned and laughed, a sound so sweet that Julia could not help but laugh along with him.

"Yes, I will come," she said, just as the window behind them fell in with a crash of glass. She blinked, just once, and then seemed to be looking down from a great height. The train was halfway across a long bridge, and already falling from the rails. Tall towers of iron buckled and bent in the wind, throwing metal and stone down to the foaming waters far below.

She remembered George's words. *The cylindrical cast iron columns supporting the long span of the bridge are each seventy-five yards long.*

"Five and seventy, three score and fifteen, a long span come to a sudden end, as they all do, in darkness and turmoil," her companion whispered.

She lay her head against his chest, listening to the thrum of his wings against the wind.

"Now tread we a measure," she said softly, as the Tay Bridge fell into the river far below.

Wings in the Firelight

by John J. Barnes

I first learned the hard truth of who I was in the winter of '76.

December is a tough month for the people of Cape Albawash, Delaware. They say if the cold doesn't make you sick, it will make you mad. And they're right. I know. I've lived here since I was a seed in my mama's womb.

The snow started coming down on Thanksgiving and didn't quit until after the year concluded. The days were gray and livid, and the nights were hardly survivable, with temperatures capable of cracking even the most work-hardened knuckles until they bled.

I was sixteen and riding out the worst case of the flu I'd ever had while Mama tended to my needs. I spent most of the month lying in bed, a serving tray full of medicine, a glass of orange juice, and a small tin wastebasket filled with my own bile by my side.

Mama brought me fresh juice and crackers every hour and emptied the throw-up in the wastebasket, thoroughly washing it out with bleach to dilute the smell. God bless her.

"You're running on empty, Miss Bellingham," Mama said. "What I saw was greener than gull doo. One more like it and we're taking a trip to the hospital."

Mama didn't like hospitals and insisted on visiting them as little as possible, having always been a firm believer in the body's ability to heal itself. She was a stout woman, strong of body and sound of mind. Her name was Emma Violet Bellingham. I'm Madeline. The two of us lived together alone, me without a father figure and Mama without a partner. Someone to lay me down to sleep at night and comfort me with a fable and tell me that everything is right in the world and that Madeline Bellingham must get her rest, for every given day is a gift.

There had been no such person. Mama never married and had only three lovers in the span of her sixty-three years. She never said which of them was my father, always said I didn't need to know. "If they felt they couldn't raise you, then they don't deserve the credit," she'd said. Fair enough, but I'd always wondered, mostly in the form of fantasies, where a DNA test might confirm that I'm the spawn of some A-list movie star or wealthy architect. I figured it couldn't hurt as long as I never learned the truth.

How wrong I had been.

Wings in the firelight.

The image came to me in . . . I didn't know what to call them. Dreams? Visions? Precognitive sight? Post-cognitive apparitions? I'd been in a recuperative state from my bout of illness, feeling better but still out of school.

The image was that of a pair of brown wings, rounded at the edges, the surfaces covered with fine fuzz and painted with black abstracts that distinctly resembled an inkblot or Rorschach test. They fluttered at rapid speed, as if whatever controlled them were in some great peril.

I saw them only as they came into an unsteady flicker of surrounding firelight.

My illness started to wane as winter pressed on. I quickly went through every book and magazine in the house as television tended to upset my delicate equilibrium. I started sketching my daydreams as I saw them in my head. Mama found them as she was serving me dry toast and tea one morning.

She studied them with great interest, and I saw in her eyes something like nostalgia. She ran her fingers gently over the paper as a widow would with a photo of her dead lover.

"Mama, you all right?"

She turned to me and smiled. Only her smile was surface deep, thinly masking the obvious turmoil stirring underneath.

Mama then looked back at the drawings. Her face remained solemn and concerned.

"What is it, Mama?"

She sat there a minute, staring at my drawing, seemingly perturbed with whatever was going through her head. I asked her a second time while shaking the hand she'd been holding me with. She snapped out of her trance.

"Nothing," she said, flashing a grin. "Just head jogging is all." But something in her eyes said she knew more than she was letting on.

Mama then served my breakfast and slipped my drawings in the top draw of the writing desk.

"Get some rest," she said, gently shutting the door behind her.

Mama said she needed to speak to me (a "red-flag talk" she liked to call the important conversations) as she was coming home from work the next evening. She worked long hours as a hospital administrator and almost always came home raccoon-eyed and exhausted. I recovered almost all of my health by then and spent the day nursing the last of a raw throat with tea and tomato soup. I was folding fresh laundry on the sofa and watching *Looney Tunes*.

"Sure," I said, snapping off the television, cutting off Bugs Bunny in the middle of one of his witty quips.

Mama set her handbag and corduroy coat by the door and walked to the couch and clutched the arm. She asked me how my day was, and

I quickly said fine, anxious to get to the root of the matter.

"Do you remember when you were really little?"

"A little, mainly our trip to the zoo." I shuddered at the thought, but Mama snickered and blushed. And she had good reason to: when I was five, I leaned too far into a monkey cage and got my head stuck. It'd taken twenty minutes and three men to pry me free. A crowd formed around me, watching and laughing as Colobus and Spider monkeys took turns chewing on my ears and slapping me in the face.

"What about your dreams? Do they tell you anything besides what you see?"

I thought about it for a minute, then said no. The visions had always been brief and ambiguous, showing me just enough to tickle my curiosity.

"Maddie," she said, tipping her head. "You're going through changes you might not fully understand . . ."

"Is this 'the speech', mama? Because I already know. We learned it in school."

"To which subject are you referring?"

"On becoming a woman."

She smiled and shook her head. "No, it's not that, Madeline."

I asked her what it could be.

"You're very special, Maddie. So special that you will see and know and do things no one else can."

I asked her why.

She licked her lips, seeming to gather her thoughts. "When I conceived you, I hadn't been with a man for quite some time. I dreamt of white light and the shadow of a figure that was in them."

She reached into the pocket of her white hip-huggers and pulled out a folded and stained piece of paper. She unfolded the sheet and held it out to me.

It was a familiar depiction of my winged man, obscured by its artist's abstract style. Written in the corner was this: E.V. Bellingham '59.

"The same as your drawings."

I looked at her, scared and confused.

"He spoke to me, said that I would be with child soon. And then you came."

"Is he—"

"I don't know who or what he is, but I believe he is special, just like you are special. I wanted a child and he knew this, but somewhere, deep down, I believe he wanted one, too."

"What am I supposed to do?"

There was silence, and the look on Mama's face told me that she was just as scared and confused as I.

"As your mother, I wish I had the words to prepare you for whatever is going to happen, but truth be told, I don't know myself. I can only tell you what my mother told me when life got too big: trust your instincts. God gave them to us for a reason, and they're usually never wrong."

Mama tucked me into bed that night and told me all was right in the world and everything would work itself out. She then kissed me and turned out the light.

That night I left Madeline Bellingham asleep in her bed and became something else entirely.

I *dreamed* of worlds past, present and afar. Worlds not yet seen with the eyes of any human being on Earth but which I knew for sure were real. I saw people from all walks of time, building fires, cleaning muskets, riding in odd floating devices I knew did not yet exist. Some of them saw me as I descended in an arc for a better view, and I pulled back at their panic.

I *felt* time and light and the seed of creation pass through me as if I were without substance. The darkness was "what is" and the light was just a temporary thing striving "to be."

Shards of blue-white light, crisp as beams of sunlight shooting through clear surf, enveloped me in a kind of ethereal cocoon.

Mama walked up to me, a dark shadow on the tangible side of the chrysalis and placed her hand on its surface. I touched my carapace-sheathed claw over hers and felt her warmth.

"My child," I heard her say, and that was all.

I fell into a deep hibernation soon after. I don't know for how long, only that I had never rested so soundly before in my life.

I awoke to a vision flashing in rote: *wings in the firelight.* I opened my eyes and found that I was sifting in the clouds. And then I heard his voice; it sounded vibrant and nonhuman, like the sentient humming of a live wire. Some part of me—a newly acquired part—was drawn to it.

I made through the night with great haste, cutting wildly through the air, toward his cry. Evergreen woods surrounded me. His screeching rang in my head like a cacophony of broken violins. And then I saw it: a flood of orange light in the forest.

I dove to the forest canopy with a smooth, steady glide toward it, senses tingling with his cries. The forest opened to a clearing of ragweed and soapstone piles. The firs and conifers along its edge had been set aflame, and a mob of men stood in a circle around my caller, waving wooden bats and machetes and firing off their rifles in the air.

My caller was flying in small tight circles at the center. With my newly enhanced optics, I saw the pattern of his wings. My vision had come to life, with smell and sound and meaning.

My caller was snared in some sort of modified bear trap. His captors provoked and hollered at him, though none were bold enough to approach him. Each time they stepped forward, he'd let out a harsh baying to deter them.

I am here, I thought, and he looked up.

Everything after that happened in a blur.

I nose-dived into the clearing. One of the men shouted, "Second in the sky!" and I forced their perimeter back with an aggressive flyby, banking a curve within mere inches of their chin stubble. A few fled; most stood their ground, stirred and angered.

I made another pass; something cold and sharp pierced my side. I examined the wound and saw the handle of a steak knife protruding from my ribcage. It had only been partially thrust inside, wobbling loosely by the tip. I pulled it out, my rage heightening two-fold.

I landed between my caller—who was resting on his knees, seemingly exhausted by his own efforts to free himself—and the mob. I splayed my wingspan and glared, and I imagine my eyes brightened to an orange shine like my caller's, like the fire. The men hollered obscenities and thrust their rakes and bats and knives at me, though none of them would actually step forward to contest me.

I screamed, and a sound like flies buzzing in water emanated from my throat. A torch flew from the back of the mob and whipped just past my face. I screamed again, lunged.

"Kill it," one of the men yelled. "It's loose! Kill it!"

A bull-nosed man in a flannel shirt pointed his shotgun my way and charged. I felt the shift of his finger in the wind and swept toward him, slashing his shoulder with my appendage. He grunted, stumbled, and fell on his back.

I screeched and my eyes grew brighter as the men's faces lit up, surfacing the terror hidden under all their pride and false courage.

"Die in your beds," I whispered, and somehow they heard. "Not tonight."

The majority fled into the woods. A few remained steadfast, though once seeing how sparse their numbers had become, retreated. I approached my caller and, with our combined strength, he was free of the trap.

He stood a good three feet taller than me.

His voice came again in my head: "Madeline."

"Father?"

He nodded once, deliberately.

I had so much I needed to ask him, but didn't know where to start. We stood there in silence, unable to read each other's expressionless, insect faces.

"Don't be scared," he said, his voice gentle and airy.

"I'm not."

I was curious as to what kind of creature he was, and therefore what I was. Though I hadn't the will to ask, I could feel him in my head, reading my thoughts.

"Nothing really understands what it is, or what it's here to do. It only knows that it *is*."

Despite the ambiguity of his answer, I somehow knew what he meant. Someone is born, lives, discovers things about his or herself, uses those things and dies. Sometimes we leave our mark, sometimes not. The chain connects at both ends.

"What do you need me to do?"

"What feels right to you?" he responded.

He touched me on the shoulder with his feeler. I was galvanized with a surge of his energy, and memories from his past flashed like pictures in my head:

He speaks to a young man in a Doughboy helmet, who's shivering in a trench . . . He stands in a field of sunflowers, an old coonhound running to him to investigate his odd scent, and when he tries to pet it, its life functions cease, suddenly, like a bolt of lightning to the head . . . He stands in an old TNT factory as a young couple drive by, staring in terror . . . He weeps as a bridge painted silver collapses into a river, bringing screaming voices locked in the cabs of automobiles with it.

"Forty-two," he said. "Nothing is infallible."

"But it wasn't your fault," I said.

"I speak; they do not listen."

"Then why do you try?"

"Because, even the nonbelievers are part of the balance." He blinked and his eyelids made a distinct squishing sound. "As for you, dear Madeline, thank you for coming for me when you did."

I thought about what he said, *when you did,* and I still think about it. It seemed my metamorphosis had come at the opportune time, as if he knew about his capture and allowed it to take its course anyway. I asked him why.

"Because all things must observe the balance, even me."

He spread his wings in preparation for flight. I put up my appendage. "Wait. Will I ever see you again?"

"I don't see why not," he said, and then he was gone.

Wildlife and Game showed up soon after he left, along with the Cape Albawash fire department. They set in to dousing the flames and stopped when they caught sight of me, staring in disbelief with their hoses and cranks in hand. I took off and disappeared under cover of night, watching the stars as I flew.

It pained me to think of my life ahead, however long that may be, as a keeper of the balance. A life of eternal selflessness as an agent to whatever power lay in the void. I would live for everything and keep nothing for myself. A solitary life. I suppose that would've been all right had I not been born a human first, with the balance being all I'd ever known or needed, but as it turns out, I wasn't. A bigger part of me needed to live for something more, to feel warmth and love and pain and companionship.

I descended on the front lawn of my house as light as a falling feather, and a strange thing started to happen. My body itched and I started shedding my insect flesh.

The lights were all off in the house except for the mini-lamp in my bedroom. I walked toward it as if it were a beacon. Every step closer brought a chunk or two to fall to the grass, where it decomposed like ice on a hot sidewalk.

I'd made my decision, and whatever part of me I'd received from my father had accepted that and stripped me of my gifts, of my moth-flesh, probably to be salvaged in the void.

The thick outer surface of my head split like the rind of a coconut, releasing my human face, which was wet with a slick, filmy gelatin. I rubbed my eyes and breathed deeply as I arriving at the window. Mama was sleeping in my bed, my stuffed giraffe cradled in her arms.

Her eyes opened slowly as if she had felt my presence. And then she smiled at me. Standing there in the lawn, naked and covered with plasma from my discarded insect body, I smiled and placed my hand on the window.

Mama said something, and even though I couldn't hear her through the glass, I read the movement of her lips. "Welcome home," she'd said.

Behind His Smile, A Frown

By Adrian Ludens

There are only three of us staying in this dilapidated little roadside motel. It's a sad indicator of the shortened attention spans of people today. There was a time when—thanks to the Mothman legend—this motel would be flashing their 'no vacancy' sign for most of the year.

The man in number twelve interests me a great deal. We've passed each other twice, crunching across the motel's dusty parking lot. He glanced down at me and offered a tentative smile as we passed, and I nodded cordially in return, but that was all. His appearance was initially rather off-putting, but I've decided I would like very much to visit with the guy. His presence is the one interesting thing in this dreary place. The only other guest is an elderly woman who has checked in to room six. With me staying in room two, it makes me wonder if the clerk made a conscious decision to keep us as far apart as possible. Could the walls really be that thin? Perhaps they are; I've made frequent trips to the soda machine on the far side of the motel, and every time I've passed the closed door of number twelve, I can hear the tall man speaking. He says things I can't quite grasp, poses questions I have no answer for. It's like trying to follow a conversation with an astrophysicist who barely has a handle on the English language. I almost wonder if he's crazy.

But what if the man in twelve is here for the same reason I am? He might also be marking the anniversary of the first sighting of the Mothman. Plenty of people have heard about the mysterious creature, but precious few seem to be interested this year.

I mentioned the man's incessant muttered questions, but I suppose it's his eccentric appearance that most people would remember. He's very tan and quite tall, quite my opposite in these respects. His long, dark hair is combed back, and he habitually wears a glittering green full-length trench coat. I've never seen him without it. He wears a wide black belt that matches his deep-set eyes. Now that I think about it, when he smiled at me that first time, I thought he rather looked like Ozzy Osbourne. If you've seen the self-proclaimed Prince of Darkness leering from the stage in his black trench coat, then you have a fair idea of the man in room twelve.

The motel is a throwback to the heyday of Route 66 when men still wore hats. The rooms form an L shape. The office squats apart, close to the curb. My room is shabby and exudes a musty odor that I imagine spans back decades. It's the type of place one imagines has seen better days, but even those days weren't much to celebrate. The prices are quite reasonable however, and the sweaty, morbidly obese man who tends the motel office was quick to volunteer directions to the nearest gentlemen's club, which I understood was meant as a friendly gesture. I asked the clerk, who introduced himself as Dewey, about the Mothman, but he only shrugged.

"Just moved here about a month ago. Never heard of no Moss Man."

He seemed sincere so I didn't bother to correct him.

A vacant strip mall squats next to the motel on one side, and a decrepit warehouse leans in from the other. Drive a few miles north of here on Route 62 and you'll encounter the abandoned remnants of the West Virginia Ordnance Works. Travel a mite farther and lose yourself in the McClintic Wildlife Area. I suppose it's not a typical tourist destination. But I'm not a typical tourist. Nor—I am willing to wager—is the man in twelve.

I wonder if we are pilgrims still searching for the truth about the

Mothman. If I could devise a way of conversing with the grinning man, we might share our experiences and anecdotes with each other.

I've been here over a week and if there's a friendly or talkative person besides the corpulent motel clerk in this town, I haven't met them yet. Although the waitresses and store clerks accept my business—and my cash—readily enough, they pretend not to hear my questions concerning the Mothman. I find their collective silence rather perplexing. Much to my surprise, the statue depicting a rather sensationalized artist's rendition of the Mothman has been taken down. Gone are all the souvenirs. Truth be told, I can find no trace of the legend, though I know it exists. I wonder at this sudden change.

I habitually drive my car around town and the surrounding area, wandering and exploring each day until late into the evenings. The cherished notion that I might miraculously encounter the Mothman is never far from my mind.

In fact, as I turned into the motel parking lot after another disappointing and uneventful day, a strange figure froze in the glare of my headlights. My heart leapt into my throat. *The Mothman!*

But no. My eyes had deceived me. I hit the brakes and stopped only inches from the tall man from twelve. Despite the close call, he grinned when he recognized me. His green duster sparkled in the illumination and billowed behind him in the breeze like wings. No wonder I'd been briefly fooled. The dark man nodded at me—still grinning—and strode quickly across the lot. My radio erupted with crackling bursts of feedback from several stations, all talk radio programs by the sounds of it. I fumbled with the volume knob, but the sounds seemed to diminish of their own accord. I glanced up in time to see the tall man push open the door to room ten and disappear inside. Surprised, I drove the last few yards in uneasy silence.

I wonder if the man in the green duster is here without transportation. I have yet to run into him at any of the diners or convenience stores around town. I've even described him a few times—I assumed a fellow that eccentric looking was bound to get local tongues wagging—but all I got were blank stares in return.

He must not have been satisfied with room ten, either. I could hear him running through the litany of his incessant questions as I passed room eight this afternoon on my way to the soda machine. I felt half-tempted to simply knock on his door and use his room-hopping as an excuse to start a conversation, but I chickened out again and kept moving. Headaches seem to arise with each trip to the vending machines, but I can't decide if it's more or less caffeine my body craves.

This is just morbid; the man with the perpetual grin now occupies room six.

An ambulance arrived early this morning, and a pair of sleepy attendants wheeled the old woman out on a collapsible gurney and hoisted her body into the back of the vehicle. I say 'body', because if she were alive they certainly wouldn't have zipped her into that telltale black bag for the trip.

The motel clerk didn't know the cause of her passing, even after I had offered him a ten-dollar bill for his trouble, so I again took him at his word.

As I climbed into my car the next morning, I sensed someone watching me and looked up. The new occupant of room six stood in the window parting the curtains and grinning at me. He acted as if he and I were sharing some ghoulish secret, and I felt my heart start to race. I backed out and sped away down Route 62.

Today, while hiking in the McClintic Wildlife Area, I had a chance encounter with a park ranger. The fresh air cleared my head, and I felt great, as I often did out in the open fresh air. I'd been wandering along a nature trail, and the ranger marched in my direction from deeper in the brush. We exchanged greetings and mild pleasantries. His name, he said, was Simon. He said he was making the rounds to ensure the deer hunters were following the appropriate laws.

"Need a special permit to hunt out here," Simon said. "Only bucks with an antler span of fourteen inches or greater can be kilt."

He pronounced 'killed' with a 't' at the end, which somehow put me at ease. Whatever coldness had infected most of the town hadn't affected the park ranger; at least, as far as I could tell. I broached the subject of the Mothman.

"Wasn't a moth, wasn't a man," Simon said. He hitched up his belt in a way that reminded me of Barney Fife. "It was a bird."

"I'll be darned. Must've been pretty big."

"Oh, it was," Simon said. He leaned in and lowered his voice though we were alone. "My daddy was a park ranger here in the sixties and seventies. He passed on in '82 but told me the truth about the Mothman a few days before he died." I held his gaze and waited.

"The Mothman was really a mutated bird, probably a giant Sandhill Crane. The thing had two necks and two heads! My daddy swore to the fact on his deathbed. Said the thing had a wingspan of almost thirteen feet. He thinks the red foreheads accounted for the red glowing eyes folks claim they saw."

"How'd a giant two-headed crane disappear like it did?" I asked. I was starting to think there might be something to Simon's story.

"Just a few days after some folks saw it roosting on the Silver Bridge, it flew into a power line. Blew out the 'lectricity in Point Pleasant and burned into a crispy critter. Animal control called in the Park Service to have a look-see. What was left of the bird stunk to high heaven and was barely recognizable. The feathers had melted together like wax. My father said they'd kept the bird spread out on the concrete floor of one of the old ordnance buildings at the TNT factory for just a day before it decomposed into ash." He shook his head as if to clear it. "Happened so fast that no one ever got a picture of it, but it was a bird. I'd swear on my daddy's grave."

"I'm sure that won't be necessary," I said. "Nice chatting with you." We shook hands and parted.

I arrived back at the motel to discover the grinning mystery man had turned the corner and now occupied room four.

Not that I should have been surprised. I would have been more astonished had he *not* moved. I've almost given up on understanding his eccentric actions and simply accepted them. Given the grand scheme of things, constantly switching rooms at a seedy motel isn't unheard of. Maybe he's just bored. Or he could be trying to find a cleaner room. I haven't seen a maid or housekeeper since I checked in.

Still, there is something decidedly foreign in his manner. Take his odd clothing, for instance, or the unceasing stream of questions I hear every time I pass his room. What would a conversation with the grinning man entail?

I feel hungover though I didn't do any drinking last night. This morning I awoke face down on the worn and musty fibers that pass as carpet here and staggered to the bathroom sink to splash my face. I tossed and turned all night. The noise from room four had me gritting my teeth and wrapping the lumpy pillow around my ears. When I did manage to drift away my sleep was plagued with nightmares.

"Drovizel! Where is you?" The voice had sounded like it belonged to a chain-smoking caveman filtered through an old drive-in movie speaker. The sound had scrambled my brain like a relentless fever dream. *"They bolted. I lost them. Drovizel, where is you?"* If the sound had gotten any louder I thought the grimy mirror in the bathroom would shatter. That or my eardrums would explode. Suddenly, the motel room door had burst open and a sparkling green figure towered in the doorway.

The mysterious man's dark eyes scanned the room. Never in my life have I seen such a haunted, ghastly face. *"Drovizel, is you here?"* he cried out as he raked his long fingers through inky black hair.

I realized two things in quick succession. First, that the man's lips were not moving as he spoke. Then I realized I wasn't asleep.

I've stayed in bed all day today. I'm not by nature a hypochondriac, but right then I believed something must be wrong with me. Or maybe lack of sleep was simply making me paranoid. Dewey somehow squeezed through his office door and waddled across the parking lot to check on me. Sweat droplets jettisoned off my shaking body and pattered onto the carpet as I stood leaning against the doorframe, listening to what he had to say. He wanted me to seek medical attention. I told him that I simply had a bug and would be fresh as a daisy in no time. I felt guilty for lying. He was probably afraid of having a second guest die at his motel in less than a week. I was afraid of leaving before I could unravel the mystery of the motel's only other occupant.

The rest of the morning, the grinning man in the sparkling green duster subjected me to a barrage of questions that my mind could not grasp. My nose bled intermittently and my head hurt so badly a migraine would be an improvement. The man had introduced himself to me several hundred times over. His name was Indrid Cold.

Around noon I gave up trying to rest and summoned all of my strength. I hoist myself out of bed. Indrid Cold's voice reverberated in my head as I staggered across the gravel to the motel office. Dewey looked up in surprise and reached for his old wall-mounted phone. I held up a hand.

"You can call an ambulance after you answer a couple questions for me." I paused to catch my breath. Indrid wasn't as audible here. The motel clerk nodded.

"You hear that television blasting all the time?"

"Nossir."

"Hear anyone yelling or talking?"

The clerk shook his head.

"Dewey, you ever serve in Vietnam or anything?"

The obese man just looked at me like I was crazy.

"What I mean is, have you got a metal plate or something in that melon of yours?"

Dewey's expression became a mix of delight and dismay, like I'd just offered him a box of chocolate-covered cockroaches. "I was in a bad car wreck two years ago," he said. He rapped his knuckles on the back of his skull. I nodded.

"Second question," I continued. "What do you know about the man in room four?"

The clerk stared at me blankly. "Four is vacant."

"Mr. Cold is in there now. He was in room twelve when I first checked in, but he's been making his way down—"

Dewey shook his head. "You're the motel's only guest."

"I've seen him several times! I hear him rambling on like a lunatic every day!" I leaned against the counter. "He's been changing rooms and getting closer to mine!"

The clerk raised his chubby hands. "You're crazy, man! You got a fever or something."

I spun around and tottered out of the office. My walk back to my room was like climbing a mountain in the face of a storm, but I pushed on. I needed closure.

I know Indrid Cold does not intend harm. I feel his sorrow and his confusion. I believe he may have gone mad. And Indrid Cold is a stranger in this world. I believe he lost something of great sentimental value a long time ago. My mind visualizes a beloved and cherished pet scampering away from a station wagon during a family vacation in a remote wilderness, and I can almost understand what went on.

The mood of the townies makes more sense, too. As Indrid Cold rambles about, he inundates minds with endless headache-inducing questions. The locals—some consciously, some not—have developed a Pavlovian response. By denying the Mothman's existence and shutting it out of their thoughts, they've found that Cold tends to leave them alone. Yet I think about the Mothman constantly. The old woman in six probably died of a brain hemorrhage when Indrid Cold got too close for too long. I blame myself. My interest in the Mothman legend somehow drew Indrid Cold to me and she paid the ultimate price as a result.

Why he chose to approach me room by room down the length of this dilapidated motel I cannot explain. And does he realize the damage he is capable of doing just by trying to communicate? If Indrid Cold sees me as a kindred spirit and has the urge to confide in me, I will not deny him. A frown of anguish hides behind his perpetual smile, and I believe I understand why. I try to remember the details Simon the park ranger shared with me. Indrid Cold will want to know them. Perhaps he'll finally find some measure of peace.

I stand at the door of room two. *My room.* My brain feels like it wants to boil out of every orifice in my head. During the brief time that I was gone, Indrid Cold has moved in. I am his ultimate goal. I steel myself and turn the knob. When the door swings open I hope I will be able to return his trademark grin.

Money Well-Earned

By Joseph Nassise

I make my living killing things.

Sometimes I kill animals. Big ones, usually. Rhinos. Elephants. Stuff like that.

More often than not, though, I kill people.

Somebody knows something they shouldn't know. Somebody sees something they aren't supposed to see. Someone else wants to make certain that they don't talk about it. That kind of thing.

It's not a bad job, as jobs go, and I'm very good at it. One of the best, actually. And that's not my ego talking, either, just a simple statement of fact. The Marine Corps trained me well, way back when, and the years I've spent since as a private contractor have honed those skills even more. I can kill a man at a thousand yards, with the right equipment and time to set up the shot. Believe you me, that's not an easy thing to do.

So I wasn't surprised when I got a message that Big Al Dantoni wanted to see me. I'd done some work for Big Al in the past. He always paid on time and never argued about the price. I like that in a guy. Straight up, ya know?

Big Al was in Vegas, so as soon as I got the message I made the necessary arrangements and caught the first flight out. Philly to Vegas, with a stop in Phoenix just to be certain I didn't have a tail. I wasn't expecting one, but it never hurt to be cautious. And I'd made a career out of being cautious.

I caught a cab at the airport and twenty-five minutes later, I was being ushered into Big Al's living room. He lived in this big place outside the city, more a compound than a house, really. Word was that

Bugsy Siegel himself had built the place back in the thirties, when those guys were throwing cash all over the place like it was going out of style. Back before RICO and federal racketeering statutes and all that.

Big Al was somewhere in the neighborhood of three hundred fifty pounds, but he moved with the grace of a man half his size. He came forward to shake my hand and gestured for me to take a seat.

He wandered over to the bar. "Drink?"

I shook my head. "I'm good."

"Mind if I have one?"

That was Big Al. Always polite. Until you ticked him off and he had some guy like me put a slug through your eye from a few hundred yards out. "Your house," I said with a slight grin. He'd been offering for ten years, and I'd be saying no just as long. It was a familiar ritual. Our way of saying, "Good to see you," or something like that.

Through a variety of cut-outs, Al ran all the construction that took place within the city limits, small and large. If you wanted to build a new hotel or casino complex, or simply wanted to add a room to your house, you went through Al. If you didn't, bad things started happening at your job site. Crew members got hurt. Tools went missing. Product showed up damaged or not at all.

Al poured himself a scotch, a generous one, and wandered back over to take a seat opposite my own.

"I've got a job for you."

That much was obvious, so I kept my mouth shut and waited to hear the rest.

"It's in West Virginia."

I shrugged.

A slight grin crossed his face. He reached down beside his chair, picked up a file, and handed it to me.

It was full of old newspaper clippings, police reports, even a few first-hand accounts written in pen on fading paper. They told an interesting story.

Late in the evening of November 15, 1966, two young couples encountered a strange creature near the abandoned TNT plant outside of Point Pleasant, West Virginia. The creature was described as being shaped like a man, but bigger, in the neighborhood of seven feet tall. It had large red eyes and a pair of monstrous wings that it kept folded against its back. When the couples sped away from the scene, the creature took to the air and followed them right up to the town limits.

Other people saw the creature that night and during the course of the next few weeks. Many of them were reputable individuals, which gave their testimony added credence. The creature, dubbed the Mothman after a villain on the popular Batman television show, was reported as either grey or dark brown and had a tendency to glide when it was aloft. Other strange occurrences were also noted during that time: odd lights in the sky, unexpected problems with televisions and telephones, cars stalled for no reason while passing by the old TNT plant.

The events continued right up until the night of December 15, 1967. On that evening the bridge that crossed the Ohio River outside Point Pleasant abruptly collapsed, killing forty-four people. Some later theories suggested that the Mothman had come to warn the people of the disaster ahead, but that his message hadn't been understood and the people of Point Pleasant, West Virginia, had paid the price.

Whatever the reason, the Mothman wasn't seen again after that fateful night.

I finished reading and tried to collect my thoughts. I was confused and not too embarrassed to say so.

"I'm sorry. I don't understand," I said, looking up.

He smiled. "Your target is right there."

"Who? Someone in these old clippings?" I started leafing through the photocopies again, paying attention to the names, looking for one that made sense given what I knew about Al's business practices.

Then a fat finger entered my frame of vision and came to rest on the picture of the artist's representation of the Mothman. The finger tapped the photo, once, and then Big Al pulled his hand back.

You have got to be kidding me. . . .

I kept my cool. "Let me get this straight. You want me to go to West Virginia. Track down a flying. . ." I glanced down at the paper to get the name right, "Mothman, and bring it back here for you."

He nodded. "Yes, that's exactly right."

In the back of my head I knew that ticking Big Al off was a very bad career move, so I tried to be diplomatic about it. "Al, these articles are more than thirty years old. Since you don't have any newer ones, I'm assuming this Mothman thing hasn't been seen since 1967. The trail is cold, Al, real cold."

His grin got wider, if that was at all possible. He reached down beside his chair and handed me a second file. This one had a couple of recent articles in it from the same paper. They told of lights in the sky and the sighting of a strange figure at night just off Highway 62.

"It's happening all over again," Big Al said. "Which means he's coming back. Except this time it will be different."

He clapped his hands together like a delighted child.

"This time you'll be waiting for him."

He's gone absolutely nuts, I thought to myself. I came within a hairsbreadth of turning him down flat, right then and there, but after a moment I started to think about the financial opportunity in front of me.

Al was paying me to go to West Virginia and hunt a mythical creature that hadn't been seen in over thirty years. That meant my daily rate for as long as it took to get the job done, plus expenses. I could probably add in another 10% for hazardous duty pay, too, as there was no way of knowing how dangerous this thing was or what it might be able to do. It was simple math. Added risk equaled a higher price.

I laid it out for him, step by step. How I'd have to observe things for awhile, get the lay of the land. How it would take time to confirm whether the sightings were real or just some country BS. How, if they were the real thing, I would then need to figure out the best way of taking this thing down. I'd have to be thorough and I'd have to be sure; I probably wouldn't get more than one chance to blow it out of the sky.

He listened, nodded a few times, and handed over an envelope stuffed full of cash. "First two weeks pay plus a generous amount for expenses. I'll have a special refrigerator truck on call twenty-four hours a day to pick up the body once you've handled your end of the job."

And just like that, I became the first hit man in the history of violent crime to be hired to kill a myth.

Sometimes this job is just strange.

West Virginia was about what I expected. Lots of trees. Lots of green. Lots of long, lonely stretches of highway. After flying back from Vegas, I'd loaded my Expedition with the equipment I needed and driven south. Interstate 81 took me all the way to I-70 west, which carried me into West Virginia. At that point I switched over to 68, continuing west and crossing half the state before turning south on 79. Another two hours of travel took me into Charleston, where I stopped and had a quick lunch before completing the final leg north into Point Pleasant.

It was a quiet community, perched on the edge of West Virginia with the mighty Ohio River at its back. Population just over 4000. As I drove through the town, scoping things out and getting my bearings, I came to the conclusion that little had changed in the fortysome-odd years since the Mothman's first appearance.

Except for the statue, that is.

It was a large, silver thing, with big wings and red eyes, and was humanoid in appearance. It stood on a pedestal right there in the center of town, with a plaque commemorating that first sighting back in 1966. The statue had been done by a local sculptor, a guy by the name of Bob Roach, and I wondered for a moment if he'd ever seen the thing or if he'd just decided this was what a Mothman should look like.

Probably the latter, I thought to myself.

Turns out the town not only had a statue of their favorite monster, but a museum and an annual festival devoted to him as well. Clearly someone somewhere along the way had the bright idea to capitalize on their notoriety and would probably still be doing so fifty years from now.

That was when I made up my mind.

I knew it was crazy, but I decided then and there to act as if the Mothman was a real target. Big Al was paying me a lot of money and it didn't seem fair to write it all off without checking to see if there was any substance to it.

I needed a place to set up watch. Someplace that was out of the way enough that I wouldn't be noticed by the locals but that had a better than even chance of letting me catch it in the act, if it actually did exist.

The old TNT plant seemed to be my best bet.

The area around the plant comprised several hundred acres of dense woods. Large concrete domes were scattered here and there. The domes had held high explosives during World War II and had fallen into disrepair not too long afterward. A network of tunnels stretched throughout. I imagine it would look something like a giant ant colony, if it could be viewed in a cross-section.

Searching the place was out of the question, and it wasn't because I was worried about encountering the Mothman. There were enough natural dangers to keep me out of a place like that all on its own. Collapsing tunnels, old pitfalls, rats and other vermin. You needed a team with plenty of rope and a strong GPS signal to do it right, neither of which I had at the moment.

So instead, I set up camp in a thicket on the edge of a slender valley leading to the plant. With a wide area in front and plenty of ground cover to hide in, I would be able to see the Mothman as it was silhouetted against the open sky above. I had my favorite rifle with me, a Remington M24, fitted with a Leupold scope. A memento of my service days. I was confident that if the Mothman put in an appearance, I could shoot it out of the sky with that weapon. Easier than shooting fish in a barrel.

Except the Mothman didn't make an appearance.

At least, not for me. Other folks were seeing him left and right. Soaring across the fields. Standing by the side of the road. Just about everywhere else but the old TNT plant where it had taken up residence the first time around. Every time I went into town I'd hear the latest story, how *so and so had seen such and such* and *what did it all mean?*

Rumors were rampant. What was the Mothman trying to tell them? What disaster was going to befall the community this time? Even the authorities had gotten into the game, with work crews sent out to examine the piling beneath the Silver Bridge, checking for any sign that there might be a repeat of the original disaster.

And still I didn't see a thing.

I vowed that I would spend one more night watching the sky around the old TNT plant and then it was time for a new plan of attack.

It was the first moonless night since I'd arrived. The lights of the town didn't reach this far out and the sky around me was ablaze with stars. I was looking up at them, trying to remember the names of the constellations just to pass the time, when a dark shadow blotted out the stars above me. It was there for just a moment and then it was gone.

But there was no doubt in my mind what I had seen.

I brought my rifle to my shoulder and waited.

It would come back.

I was *sure* of it.

I watched that patch of sky for a full twenty minutes before admitting to myself that I had missed it for the night. I was disappointed, but filled with a strange sense of exultation, too. The darned thing really did exist!

I lowered the rifle and turned around, my thoughts whirling.

The Mothman stood less than a foot away, its wings stretched out above us, its red eyes glowing in the near darkness.

I knew I'd never make it, but I tried anyway.

I swung the rifle up, my finger reaching for the trigger.

The barrel wasn't even halfway to my waist when the Mothman reached out and placed one clawed hand on my shoulder.

An explosion of color and sound filled my head.

I chose a patch of high ground roughly four hundred yards from where I knew my target would appear. It was far enough away that I could get in and out again without being seen, but close enough that the wind and the natural curvature of the earth wouldn't put too much stress on the shot. I could hit a dime at four hundred yards; I wasn't worried about hitting a target as big as this one from that distance.

I settled in to wait.

It didn't take long.

The target filled the frame of my scope. Thanks to the optics, it looked close enough to touch. I squeezed the slack out of the trigger. Breathed in. Breathed out. Felt my heart beating. Once. Twice. Three times.

In the space between heartbeats, I pulled the trigger.

The gun kicked and roared.

The bullet entered Big Al's head just in front of his ear and exited out the other side in an explosion of blood, brains, and skull fragments. He was dead before his body hit the street.

As chaos broke lose on the street below me, I calmly left position and returned to my vehicle. The half-built parking garage had been a good choice. I'd had an unlimited field of fire and easy access to and from my vehicle. I was six blocks away before the first patrol car even made it to the scene.

Those who claimed the Mothman was a warning of disaster to come were right. I knew it from first-hand experience. I'd seen it all through the Mothman's touch.

The shiny new hotel and casino complex, all eighty-eight stories of it.

The shoddy materials that were used in building the hotel's foundation, because the owners refused to meet Big Al's monetary demands and he intended to teach them a lesson in obedience.

The devastating collapse of the main tower that killed three hundred and twenty-nine individuals, including fifty-seven schoolchildren there for a spelling bee.

With one shot, I kept all that from happening.

Big Al had hired me to kill a monster.

And with the Mothman's help, I'd done that *very* thing.

Afterword

By Thomas F. Monteleone

Okay, a few declarations before we get into the red meat of this piece.

1) I've always had a warm place in my heart for the Mothman because of my connection to his main investigator/champion, John A. Keel—as you will soon discover.

And

2) I have not read any of the stories in this book and, that said, am neither qualified nor inclined to comment upon their quality or any aspect of their verisimilitude to the Real Mothman.

But that's not gonna stop me. It's gonna be fun, I promise, so let's proceed, okay?

Although Keel's book, *The Mothman Prophecies*, appeared in 1975, I had actually been privy to firsthand knowledge of the Mothman only months after the strange being had been initially encountered in West Virginia. It was 1967 and I was sitting in my college apartment with none other than John A. Keel, who was a youngish, goateed journalist who also called himself a "ufologist."

The reason a UFO investigator had dropped by to

see me is the subject of several of my MAFIA columns (collectively entitled "Keep Watching the Skies!") and if any of you are suffused with a burning need to read them, you can check out the last three chapters of my omnibus collection, *The Mothers And Fathers Italian Association* or look up issues 43, 44, and 45 of *Cemetery Dance* magazine.[1]

Suffice, for purposes of brevity, to say that I perpetrated a bit of hoax (telling people I'd been contacted by aliens) and when word of my "story" got out to the underground army of flying saucer investigators, I became a subculture celebrity at the age of twenty-one. I was getting interviewed by a lot of interesting (and sometimes a little scary) guys.

That's why I wasn't all surprised when I received a call from a guy named John Keel, who wanted to assess my alleged encounter with some humanoids from the planet Lanulos. I checked him out. Keel was a legitimate writer with several books to his credit, with reputation of being a hard-nosed journalist. He was supposed to have a very good BSometer, and had no trouble unveiling many of the "contactees" he interviewed as liars.

Right from the start, I could tell this guy was highly suspicious of my story. Keel gave every indication of being clear thinking, intelligent, and erudite. He most likely walked in the door assuming I was a wise-guy college kid who was having a big laugh at the expense of a gaggle of gullible mooks.

That he'd been absolutely *correct* didn't deter me

from my appointed task of making him believe me. In fact, I respected John Keel for his accomplishments and his reputation as a somewhat skeptical investigator of things paranormal, and considered it a real challenge to see if I could turn him.

So we sat down in the living room to what had become a familiar tableau—a ufologist on the couch with his tape recorder and notepads fanned across our coffee table, and me sitting in the easy chair spinning my yarns, while my roommates drifted in and out of the room, smirking and mugging beyond the purview of the outsiders.

John Keel has done his homework, and had thoroughly digested everything available on all of my previous interviews with all the saucer enthusiasts. He knew *all* the details of everything I'd ever told anybody, and he asked tough questions, which required someone fast on his feet and possessing access to a vast store of UFO lore, speculative science, SF, and of course, plenty of BS.

Keel came to the right place.

I fielded his queries and probes like a Dominican shortstop, throwing him out with lazy slingshot throws to first. Keel was trying to trip me up and I handled everything with finesse—answering without hesitation and plenty of confidence.

And yet, I could tell that even though this guy did NOT believe anything I was telling him, he was enjoying the mental jousting match we had going. Clearly, he did not get a chance to interrogate too many contactees who responded like me, and he was running with it. I decided the only way this evening could end would be for me to offer up something new, something I hadn't told *any* of the other investigators, something I'd been holding back because I'd been sure no one would believe me.

Something so stupendously absurd that Keel would snap off his recorder, lean back and smile as he said, "Nice try, kid. You had me going for awhile, but . . ."

Yeah, I thought. *That's exactly what I want.* That ineluctable *something* that will finally put the lid on this whole escapade, which (I finally admitted to myself) was getting tiresome. A vague idea began to take shape in the endless landscape of my imagination, rolling forward out of the mist of fabrication, to take form and, verily, substance.

So when he asked me the inevitable question (the one they always ask): was there anything else you want to tell me?—anything you haven't told anyone else? . . . I seized on the question, and I heard myself talking as if listening to another person. I marveled at the phenomenon because I had no freaking clue what I was going to say next. It was the first time I'd experienced what is now a commonplace technique I employ when writing short stories—I was telling the story to myself, I was making it up as I went along!

And, I was amazing myself.

Because as I listened to the story I was feeding Keel,

another part of my mind knew from where my subconscious was dredging up this particular prevarication.

Listen: I told John Keel, yes, there was one other thing the aliens did that was pretty weird—they *visited me in the Hot Shoppes Family Restaurant* where I had been working as a waiter several evenings per week (part of my ongoing program of working my way through college). Keel's eyebrows arched, and he leaned forward, suddenly discarding the ennui that had been slowly chewing at his edges. He spoke with an edge in his voice. "*What* did you say?"

I noticed the way he'd asked the question; he was not being sarcastic or implying anything snide. He spoke in a tone so serious, it sounded a little scary.

I repeated what I'd figured was going to be the dumbest thing I could think of, and Keel began acting a bit disquieted. "What were they wearing when they did this?"

Without missing a beat, I said: "They looked like the guys you always see in the old newsreels, you know— *men in black,* topcoats and fedoras."

"You say they were men in black?" he said softly.

"Yeah, that's what I said."

John Keel looked a bit stunned, but I pushed on, and said they told me they'd tracked me down to see if I wanted to visit their ship one last time. They said they'd be leaving and wouldn't be back for quite awhile.

By now, John Keel was getting agitated; something lurched behind his eyes, which might be perceived as true fear. I realized I'd said something which has clearly *gotten* to him, twisted him up. "Tell me every detail," he said in a whisper, underscored with grimness hard to ignore.

So, I glibly launched into a short scenario in which the humanoids wait for me to get off work, then they escort me from the Hot Shoppes to a car waiting in the parking lot, and it was of course the early-Fifties dreadnought-Packard of *Forbidden Area*, and I paused dramatically before adding this little frisson to the tale—that when I climbed into the back seat of that big, old car, *it still had that "new-car-smell"* and the engine was ticking along like a Swiss watch.

"Isn't that weird?" I say off-handedly.

John Keel had become suddenly pale, as if he'd just drafted a nice, frothy mug of botulism. He said nothing, but was clearly trying to compose himself. "Yes, it is indeed. Very Weird," he said finally in a tone like the Control Voice of *Outer Limits*. "More than you can imagine."

"Really? Whaddya mean?"

Keel leaned forward, his dark eyes drilling coresamples into me. It was a look as serious as cancer. "Last week, I was in West Virginia, checking out a complex story which involved a car *just like that one*, quite possibly the *same* car."

Okay, now it was my turn. If this had been a movie, that's where the Jagged Violins and the theramin would start doing the *Eeeeh!-Eeeeeh! Ooooo!-Ooooo!* routine over the soundtrack.

But this was no movie. It was real, and it was *my* turn to start feeling a little creeped out..How could this be possible? I was making this crap up on the fly, and Keel was telling me something like this already happened? *No freakin' way,* I thought.

But as our old pal Garth might say: *Yes-way, dude.*

Lamely, I continued my bogus story of how they drove me out to their ship on a country road in Montgomery County, Maryland, and told me they would be leaving and would not be back for many Earth-years. I described the scene: a ramp (oddly similar to the one on the ship in *Forbidden Planet*) opening in the bottom of the ellipsoid craft and the old Packard being driven up into the vast bowels of the ship. Then, I told Keel, they turned to me, shook my hand and said their goodbyes, and that I had a feeling they wouldn't be back.

"Can you remember their exact words?" asked Keel.

Now, the solemn manner in which he asked this hipped me that maybe he was looking for something significant. So I paused and acted like I was thinking very hard to reconstruct that final moment of contact between earthling and extraterrestrials.

"Well, yeah," I intoned softly. "They said: 'We'll see you in time'."

(And I knew exactly what I was doing here. . . . I purposely employed the cryptic phrasing "*in* time" to perhaps suggest that time was a palpable medium through which these guys could travel.)

And Keel, as I figured, was sharp enough to pick up

on it. He wrote out a few notes excitedly on his legal pad, then looked up at me with those drilled-out eyes. "That is very interesting. This all ties in, don't you see? This all means plenty!"

"It does?" I asked.

And Keel launched into a sort discourse on the element of "time" as being a recurrent theme in much of his recent investigations. He also advanced a clever theory as to why the aliens were dressed in black topcoats and fedoras (very unfashionable for the late Sixties) and were driving an old-year-model car—since their craft traveled at light-speeds, while little time passed inside their ships, relativistic effects and all that, many years were passing here on earth. Hence a few jaunts in and out of our atmosphere, a contact here and there during the Fifties, and several weeks were used up on board— while on Earth Buddy Holly had died, the Beatles had emerged, and Martin Luther King had been assassinated, and wham! the decade's on the way to getting wrapped by the time the Lanulesions drop in again.

Hey, I gotta give Keel credit. He knew his basic physics, and he was making an honest attempt to explain all the crapola I'd been shoveling his way.

There was a pause while we all considered what he'd been saying, and then Keel turned off his recorder and began packing up his brief case. As he did this, he revealed that before he spoke with me, he'd been convinced (as I'd figured) I was just a clever guy pulling a college prank that had spun out into something more than I'd bargained for. He was exactly right, but, hey, I wasn't going to dissuade him of what I could see was coming next.

"*But*," said Keel (and I just had a feeling there was going to be a big *But* . . .). "When you mentioned the black coats and hats and the old car, I *knew* that somehow you were telling the truth. Because those are pieces of information that no ufologist has ever released to the public. No one could know those things unless they happened."

Okay, now, I'd been sitting there feeling like I'd been written into a *Twilight Zone* script, and I knew I had to sit there a few more minutes and act righteously vindicated, but I inwardly wondered what was really going on? Keel eventually left, promising to stay in touch.

What happened next, and over the next few years, is this: Keel wrote a huge book about the whole UFO phenomenon, called *Operation Trojan Horse*, and he mentioned my case and used my real name (even though he'd agreed *not* to do so . . .). You can probably find a copy on eBay if you're that interested. I went on to graduate and eventually become a writer. Years later, I co-wrote a play called *U.F.O.!* in which I lampooned the saucer investigators, and one of the characters was a guy named Jonathan Leek. It's a funny play and the main character, a college student, ends up wondering if all the things he made up actually happened, and the aliens have given him "screen memories" to keep him from knowing of the actual events—which I have to tell you had crossed my mind (albeit fleetingly) in our *own* time-space continuum.

Okay, okay, so by now, a lot of you must be wondering what does any of this have to do with the Mothman and the stories in this book?

Good question . . .

Not a lot, actually. I just thought you would like to read another good story, although not of the fictive mode. But the main connector is John A. Keel, you see. When he told me he'd been in West Virginia investigating another case, some of the less slope-browed among you probably figured it out. Without any major ratiocination, you knew that just before seeing me, Keel had been checking out the first reports of the Mothman.

Now here's where it gets a little wonky.

John Keel eventually pulled all his data together in a book called *The Mothman Prophecies*, in which he again mentions me and my ufo/alien/contactee story. If you saw the Richard Gere film based on the book, you will recall that one of the characters is named "Leek"—the same as the character in my play.

Coincidence? I think not!

But more telling is the scene in which the Richard Gere character gets a middle-of-the-night phone call from an alien who delivers the following message: *"I'll see you in time . . ."*

(Insert alarm bells and submarine dive-klaxons here)

Yeah, right . . . so I wonder where they got *that* line

from?

Which is just another way of saying that I have been inextricably intertwined with the whole Mothman Mythos from its earliest beginnings. I have read accounts of all the reported sightings and all the additional data that suggest that the Mothman may perhaps be some sort of time-travelling entity.

Oh, and if you've been paying close attention, I think you can now go to sleep with certainty of who *really* originated the phrase *"men in black."*

See? I told you it'd be fun . . .

Thomas F. Monteleone
Fallston, MD
2011

WOODLAND PRESS, LLC

w w w . w o o d l a n d p r e s s . c o m
Now on FACEBOOK: Woodland Press, LLC
Chapmanville, West Virginia 25508
304-752-7152

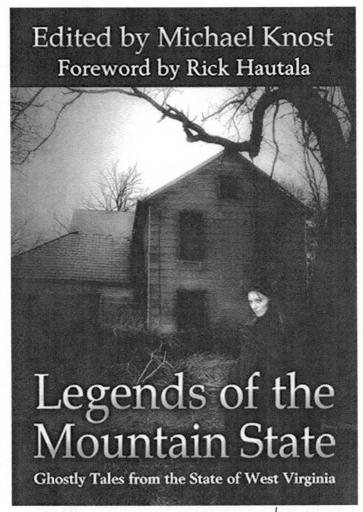

Edited by Michael Knost
Foreword by Rick Hautala

Legends of the Mountain State

Ghostly Tales from the State of West Virginia

This anthology includes thirteen accounts of ghostly manifestations, myths, and mountain mythology, based on known legends from the eerie state of West Virginia. Horror writer Michael Knost serves as the anthology's editor. Participating writers are an amalgamation of professional authors and professionals in the horror, science fiction, and fantasy fields, along with up-and-coming writers from Appalachia. Many contributors are National Bram Stoker Award winning authors currently in the national spotlight. This title is suitable for anyone who enjoys bone-chilling ghost tales told by some of the best storytellers in the business. Softcover. $18.95

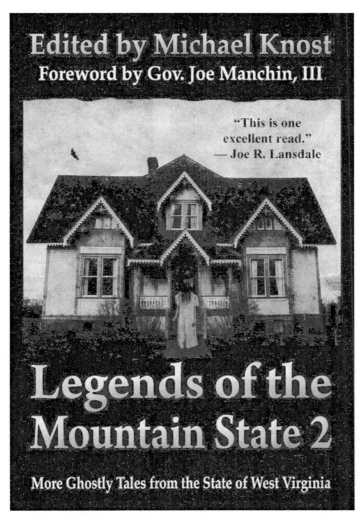

After putting together this anthology's predecessor, above, editor
Michael Knost realized he had barely scratched the surface with Appalachian folklore. After seeing great success with the initial project, Woodland Press asked Knost to put together a second edition—one that focused
on 13 additional ghost stories and mountain legends. The new project,
which is arguably even scarier than its predecessor, embodies the same
tone and texture of its forerunner, with nationally known authors and storytellers getting involved. According to Knost, this new volume offers fresh
meat to those who devoured the stories in the first volume. Softcover.
$14.95

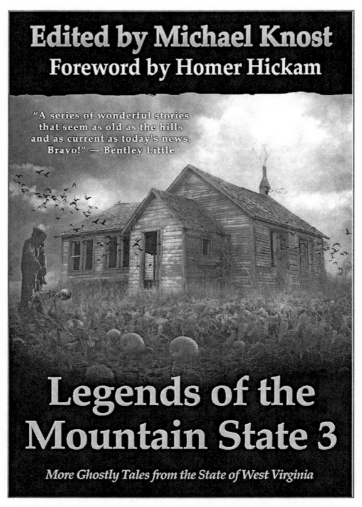

Edited by **Michael Knost**

Foreword by Homer Hickam

"A series of wonderful stories that seem as old as the hills and as current as today's news. Bravo!" — Bentley Little

Legends of the Mountain State 3

More Ghostly Tales from the State of West Virginia

The third installment of the *Legends of the Mountain State* series, above, is already being called the most amazing of the ghostly trilogy. Michael Knost again takes the reins as chief editor and coordinator. Here you'll find 13 final chapters—bone-chilling ghost tales and treacherous legends. Stories are penned by many of the preeminent writers in the business—National Bram Stoker Award winners, nationally known horror writers, and gifted Appalachian storytellers. The tone in this project is perhaps darker, tales creepier, and the overall texture even grittier than the first two installments. Foreword by beloved American author Homer Hickam. Softcover. $18.95

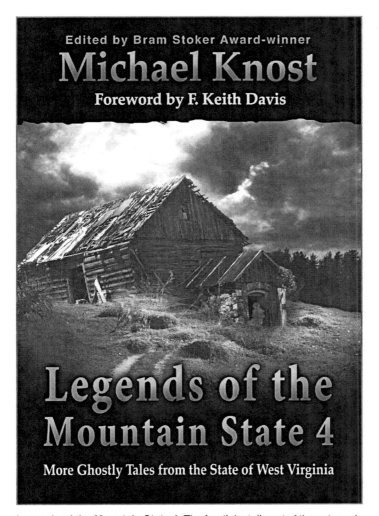

Edited by Bram Stoker Award-winner
Michael Knost
Foreword by F. Keith Davis

Legends of the
Mountain State 4
More Ghostly Tales from the State of West Virginia

Legends of the Mountain State 4. The fourth installment of the extremely popular "Legends of the Mountain State" series (Woodland Press) is here—and it's fantastic! Again, Appalachian myths, ghost tales, and folklore provide an eerie backdrop for powerful, dark, and gritty storytelling. Concerning the series, Shroud Magazine has written that myth, legend, and folklore are among the most powerful forms of storytelling, and "Legends of the Mountain State 4" will not disappoint—not one bit. Michael Knost again takes the reins as chief editor and coordinator; and here you'll discover 13 "creeped-out" chapters—bone-chilling tales and legends to delight the reader. Stories are penned by many of the preeminent writers in the horror industry along with exceptional in-state storytellers. Authors include: Gary A. Braunbeck, Steve Rasnic Tem, Alethea Kontis, G. Cameron Fuller, Jason Keene, Elizabeth Massie, JG Faherty, Brian J. Hatcher, S. Clayton Rhodes, Lisa Morton, Mark Justice, Lisa Mannetti and Michael Arnzen. Softcover. $18.95

Mountain Magic: Spellbinding Tales of Appalachia. The power of magic is the power of story. Both use illusion to illustrate the truth. Both create worlds with a few magical words. And both have the power to change us forever. The Appalachian Mountains are full of stories. And magic. In *Mountain Magic: Spellbinding Tales of Appalachia*, editor Brian J. Hatcher collects stories and poems from around the world. Thirteen authors share awe-inspiring, beautiful, frightening, and sometimes deadly, magical visions. Stories about disturbing sleight of hand, earthy fantasy, and ghostly illusion. The kind of magic found only in Appalachia. The curtain is drawn. The show begins. Time to experience *Mountain Magic: Spellbinding Tales of Appalachia*. Now, watch very closely. Softcover. $18.95

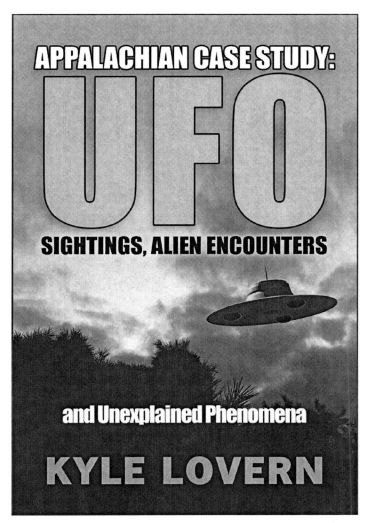

Appalachian Case Study: UFO Sightings, Alien Encounters and Unexplained Encounters. The state of West Virginia has a long prominent history of unexplained happenings and bizarre sightings of unidentified flying objects (UFOs). This fascinating literary work researches and documents sixteen unusual UFO sightings in Appalachia. The book also includes fascinating interviews with certain West Virginia citizens who have experienced the unexplainable. Author Kyle Lovern includes an exclusive interview with nationally-known and respected UFOlogist and nuclear physicist Stanton Friedman. This title has received a great deal of national attention as the focus on UFO data shifts toward Appalachia. Softcover. $12.95

APPALACHIAN CASE STUDY:

UFO

Sightings, Alien Encounters and Unexplained Phenomena

VOLUME 2

KYLE LOVERN

Appalachian Case Study: UFO Sightings, Alien Encounters and Unexplained Encounters - Volume 2. In this new release from Woodland Press. which is a sequel to a bestselling title about strange UFO sightings and bizarre alien abductions, UFOlogist Kyle Lovern focuses and broadens his scope as he researches and fully documents a variety of new UFO encounters, and revisits some famous sightings of yesteryear, that have taken place in Appalachia—in West Virginia, Virginia, Kentucky and Ohio. Softcover. $15.95

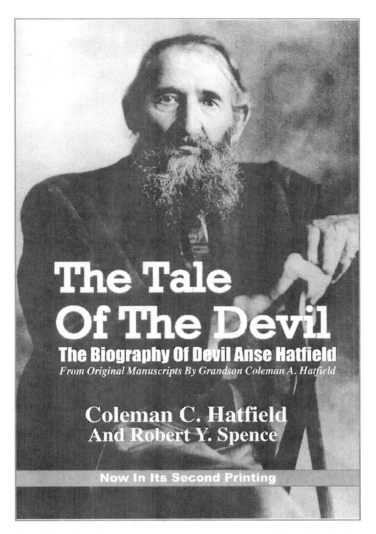

The Tale

Of The Devil

The Biography Of Devil Anse Hatfield

From Original Manuscripts By Grandson Coleman A. Hatfield

Coleman C. Hatfield
And Robert Y. Spence

Now In Its Second Printing

The Tale of the Devil represents the first biography of feudist Anderson "Devil Anse" Hatfield, written by great-grandson Dr. Coleman C. Hatfield (2004 Tamarack Author of the Year), and Mountain State historian Robert Y. Spence. Now in its third printing, this book remains an Appalachian best-seller. This biography of Devil Anse Hatfield faithfully documents his Civil War service as a Confederate soldier and leader of the fighting Wildcats militia. It tells the true story of the Hatfield-McCoy feud, the violent killings, and the post-feud years after the gunfire ceased. Handsome Commentative Hardbound. $29.95

The Secret Life and Brutal Death of Mamie Thurman. It was over seventy-eight years ago that this nasty homicide grabbed national headlines. This book takes a close look at this puzzling account. A regional bestseller, this book has been dubbed the "Hillbilly Dalia." It's a gruesome thriller and true account about a prominent, Depression era woman—a carry-over from the flapper age—found brutally and sadistically murdered in the heart of the Bible-belt. It was the last year of Prohibition. Mamie Thurman was a member of the tight-lipped, local aristocracy that frequented a private club in downtown Logan, WV—a wild speakeasy. She lived a risky lifestyle. Now new evidence points to several groups—from the mob to the KKK, from rumrunners to a slew of local merchants—as having a part in this true-crime. Softcover. $15.95

The Feuding Hatfields & McCoys. This unique book is about two proud families. *The Feuding Hatfields & McCoys* is a title that includes a comprehensive timeline of the feuding Hatfield family migration westward and documents the history before, during, and following the bloody feud era. Included are stories—which have never before been published—that have been collected from the Hatfield family over the years. These chapters add color and clarity to this famous vendetta. Author Dr. Coleman C. Hatfield was the great-grandson of Anderson "Devil Anse" Hatfield and was a noted Mountain State historian. Softcover. $18.95

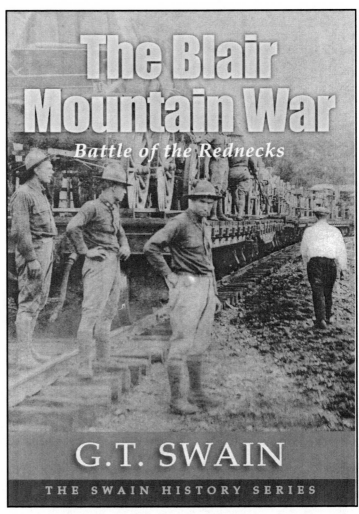

The Blair Mountain War: Battle of the Rednecks, tells the true story of the Blair Mountain War, the largest organized armed uprising in US labor history. At the time of this original manuscript, written in 1927, G.T. Swain was a reporter for The Logan County Banner, in Logan, WV. Here Swain paints a vivid picture, in his most unique style, and documents the accounts surrounding the 1921 Blair Mountain War. The WV State Archives has since stated that the mine wars have demonstrated the inability of the state and federal governments to defuse the situations short of initiating armed intervention. This is certainly true. Regardless, the details behind The Blair Mountain War remain fascinating and controversial. $12.50

Princess Aracoma and the Settling of West Virginia. Upon the tragic death of Chief Cornstalk in 1774, the Shawnees followed Cornstalk's daughter, Princess Aracoma, into present-day Midelburg Island in Logan County, West Virginia. This book aptly describes the settling of the Mountain State and explains how Princess Aracoma resolved a difficult conflict between the American Indian population and the region's earliest settlers. This title was originally authored by journalist and historian G.T. Swain in 1927. The end result is a true story and an exciting adventure, involving Indian Princess Aracoma, that takes place upon the immense backdrop of American history. $12.95

Edited By Michael Knost and Mark Justice

APPALACHIAN
WINTER HAUNTINGS

Weird Holiday Tales from the Mountains

Appalachian Winter Hauntings includes eleven bone-chilling accounts, penned by many of the preeminent storytellers in the business. These stories are appropriate to the Appalachian region and relative to the heart of the winter season. It's dark and cold and designed for cozying up close to a blazing fireplace on the coldest of winter nights. Michael Knost and Mark Justice wanted to seek unusual stories with a wintry and ghostly theme. Contributors and powerful storytellers include: Ronald Kelly, Brian J. Hatcher, Patricia Hughes, Steve Vernon, S. Clayton Rhodes, Steve Rasnic Tem, Sara J. Larson, Scott Nicholson, J.G. Faherty. EmmaLee Pallai, and Elizabeth Massie. The texture is gritty and the stories are moving and, yes, c-h-i-l-l-i-n-g. So, pour yourself a mug of hot cocoa, wrap your favorite blanket around you tight, and brace yourself for ghostly stories and weird encounters that take place in the shadows of snowy hilltops or along icy mountain trails.. Softcover. $14.95

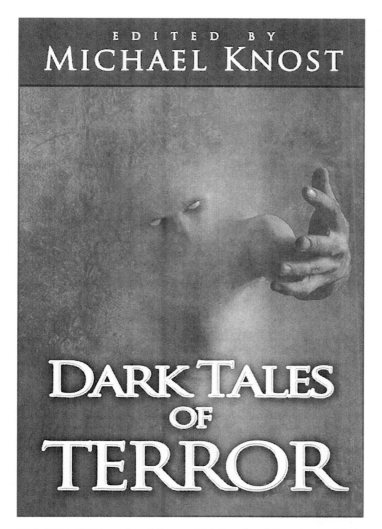

EDITED BY
MICHAEL KNOST

DARK TALES OF TERROR

Dark Tales of Terror. Brand New and totally unique! Experience sixteen bone-chilling short stories by exceptional Appalachian storytellers with strong appetites for the macabre. Within these pages lie terrifying ghost tales and strange encounters sure to cause more than a few sleepless nights. *Dark Tales of Terror* is a gripping anthology—full of Southern fried horror of the first degree—assembled by 2009 Bram Stoker Award winner Michael Knost. A number one best-seller in West Virginia and Kentucky bookstores, this book's contributors include Karin Fuller, Karen L. Newman, Lesley Conner, Miranda Phillips Walker, Jessie Grayson, Ellen Thompson McCloud, Ellen Bolt, Geoffrey Cameron Fuller, Eric Fritzius, Brian J. Hatcher, Michael Fitzgerald, S. Clayton Rhodes, Robert W. Walker, Jason L. Keene and others. Softcover. $18.95

Writers Workshop of Horror

"A veritable treasure trove of information for aspiring writers, straight from the mouths of today's top horror scribes!"
— *Rue Morgue Magazine*

"Packing more knowledge and sound advice than four years' worth of college courses... It's focused on the root of your evil, the writing itself."

— *Fangoria Magazine*

"Entertaining, informative, and also plain old fun, this book will not only make you want to write more, it will give you the tools to write better. This should be mandatory reading in creative writing classes."

— *Horror World*

2009 Bram Stoker Award winning title. Writers Workshop of Horror focuses solely on honing the craft of writing. It includes solid advice, from professionals of every publishing level, on how to improve one's writing skills. The volume edited by Bram Stoker Award winner Michael Knost includes contributions by a dream-team of nationally known authors and storytellers. Contributors to this work include: **Clive Barker, Joe R. Lansdale, F. Paul Wilson, Ramsey Campbell, Thomas F. Monteleone, Deborah LeBlanc, Gary A. Braunbeck, Brian Keene, Elizabeth Massie, Tom Piccirilli, Jonathan Maberry, Tim Waggoner, Mort Castle, G. Cameron Fuller, Rick Hautala, Scott Nicholson, Michael A. Arnzen, J.F. Gonzalez, Michael Laimo, Lucy A. Snyder, Jeff Strand, Lisa Morton, Jack Haringa, Gary Frank, Jason Sizemore, Robert N. Lee, Tim Deal, Brian Yount, and others.** Softcover $21.95

CPSIA information can be obtained
at www.ICGtesting.com
Printed in the USA
FFOW02n1801191115
18808FF